Her Kind
a novel

Her Kind
a novel

Robin Throne

918studio Press

This is a work of alternative historical fiction and the appearance of certain historical figures is therefore inevitable. All characters, however, are products of the author's imagination and any resemblance or similarities with persons living or deceased are entirely coincidental or used fictitiously.

Her Kind, a novel

5ᵗʰ ANNIVERSARY EDITION

Robin Throne

224 pages

Published by 918studio Press

ISBN-10: 0692142983

ISBN-13: 978-0692142981

Copyright © 2013, 2018 Robin Throne

Printed in the United States of America

All rights reserved

Cover and interior design Sarah Throne

"Her Kind" [poem] reprinted by permission of SLL/Sterling Lord Literistic, Inc. Copyright by Anne Sexton.

William Stafford, Ask Me from *The Way It Is: New and Selected Poems*. Copyright ©1977, 1998 by William Stafford and the Estate of William Stafford. Reprinted with the permission of The Permissions Company, Inc. on behalf of Graywolf Press, Minneapolis, Minnesota, www.graywolfpress.org.

for Emma

& all the other ghosts at 918 River Road

Foreward

Crossing the Mississippi River conjures primordial memory in any century. Searching for safety atop a volatile, fluid, or treacherous icy membrane activates a sense of life and death simultaneously as we arrive into the future with personal history undertow.

Like modern buoys defining the channel, single-page historic excerpts from The Book of Genesis, The Indian Removal Act by The Twenty-first United States Congress, The Annals of the State Historic Society of Iowa: County of Scott, Territorial Acts, and the Iowa Code regarding Void Marriages to name a few, mark time with profound social punctuation.

A mix of memory and longing artfully charted in *Her Kind* by Robin Throne navigates the collective consciousness with illuminating skill inspired by journal entries from a female pioneer. As a woman who grew up along the Mississippi River where this novel awakens, I am returned in time from the future to this place where river crossings evoke and dredge physical and emotional experiences about life, the river and being a woman.

Nancy L. Purington, MFA
Mississippi River Visual Artist
Iowa City, Iowa
Author, *Moonlight on the Mississippi*

Her Kind

I have gone out, a possessed witch,
haunting the black air, braver at night;
dreaming evil, I have done my hitch
over the plain houses, light by light:
lonely thing, twelve-fingered, out of mind.
A woman like that is not a woman, quite.
I have been her kind.

I have found the warm caves in the woods,
filled them with skillets, carvings, shelves,
closets, silks, innumerable goods;
fixed the suppers for the worms and the elves:
whining, rearranging the disaligned.
A woman like that is misunderstood.
I have been her kind.

I have ridden in your cart, driver,
waved my nude arms at villages going by,
learning the last bright routes, survivor
where your flames still bite my thigh
and my ribs crack where your wheels wind.
A woman like that is not ashamed to die.
I have been her kind.

Anne Sexton

My sister, Rose Emma Parmlee, wrote and assembled this manuscript on her deathbed in 1957. Quite amazing, considering her declining health. I have preserved it only out of respect for the one member of my family who blessed my marriage to my first cousin and loving wife, Lillie May Belle Sargent Parmlee. Please remember that we came from a good Iowa family, and these pages are simply the ranting of an aging spinster and nothing more.

H.D. PARMLEE

FEBRUARY 6, 1961

Rose's Manuscript

Moses —□ ○— Laura   Syl —□ ○— Phoebe

Henry —□ ○— Emma

Rose Emma ○—

I am 90 years young today.

They laugh as they tell me this as if it is some sort of a humorous barb that will lift my spirits. I am now certain that I will see them all again, very soon now. Perhaps then they will answer my questions, put the final pieces together of what I cannot yet know. Although I do know most of it by now and that is why I am putting it down here.

I do not feel that I will see 91, but I do not tell these guardians this today. They have tired of hearing of my age and circumstance so it is quite kind of them to remember me today.

I ask the Lord my soul to keep.

It seems so odd to me now that I had never felt fear as a child when I was told to say this prayer aloud. I recited it so mindlessly with no real passion or understanding of what it actually was for that I so resolutely prayed.

If I shall die before I wake, I ask the Lord my soul to take.

I have begun hearing my grandmothers these days. My grandfathers, too. Their voices are as real as my childhood. I remember so clearly how my grandmothers would stand over our beds.

Say your prayers now, girls.

I would like to be that child again.

Resolute.

Fearless.

Calling out death. Let it come for me now. I am ready.

Praying only for a safe passage if death should come this night.

Perhaps if it does come soon, I will finally be lifted from this life that has been just a bit too long.

Cross my heart and hope to die.

Asaph   Mary-Ann

Lillie May Belle

April 6, 1876

Ten fingers!

Ten toes!

How many times in my life would I live to hear these exclamations over a baby's birth? Never as many as my mother had.

When Mrs. Parkhurst exclaimed the digital outcome for Lillie May Belle Sargent it truly was a reason for rejoicing, and would likely be so at every birth in the Treat-Condit-Sargent-Parmlee family to come.

When Lillie May's mother, my Aunt Mary-Ann, had shown me the family tree in the fragile front matter pages of the Sargent family Bible, I was nine years old. By then I was the best reader in all of Parkhurst School, including all of the sixth graders, so I could not help but follow the asterisk that Uncle Asaph's great-aunt Martha had noted next to seven of Asaph's 13 brothers and sisters.

As Mary-Ann made the new entry to record Lillie May's birth, I carefully scanned the lineage of my mother's sister's husband.

My aunt must have thought me such an obedient and faithful child then, retreating to the east sitting room on each visit, pulling that worn King James family Bible into my lap and reviewing page after page as closely if I were the Scott County magistrate reviewing his decree for improper punctuation, so meticulous was our search.

The magistrate peering through spectacles; me, reading with the clear eyes from my Condit side. No, Mary-Ann did not caution me about tearing the fragile pages. She did not even look over my shoulder to review my reading. Perhaps she never even knew what I might find.

There it was.

In the upper left corner of the first blank page behind the book of Revelation, I found Martha's careful asterisked script:

Eleven fingers, eleven toes

Mortuary Record.

Emma Parmlee

Keen regret will be felt among the old settlers of Scott County and among all numbered in the circle of her acquaintances over the death of Mrs. Emma Parmlee, which occurred at her home on the River Road, Sunday morning. In her death the Scott County Settler's association mourns one of its earliest members and the county loses one of the best women of its pioneers.

Mrs. Parmlee was a native of Washington County, Pa., and was born Sept. 25, 1832. She came to Scott County with her parents, Sylvester G. and Phoebe Condit, in 1835, the family settling on the large farm in Le Claire township on which resides the only member of the family now living, Mrs. Asaph (Mary-Ann) Sargent. March 14, 1850, she was united in marriage to Henry Parmlee and for nearly half a century their home has been in the Township. Of the 11 children born to them but four survive – Rose Emma, Anna Viola, Clara Belle, and Harry Deacon, all at home with their father.

In her girlhood days the deceased became a member of the Presbyterian church and for 55 years was a consistent communicant. Mrs. Parmlee had been in declining health for the past 15 years, her final illness covering a period of eight weeks, four of which she was confined to her bed. The end came quietly and suddenly at the hour stated—a painless and peaceful passing away of one whose life here began with the settlement of this section.

The funeral will be held Wednesday at 11 o'clock from the home and the interment will be in Pioneer Cemetery.

They cannot blot out my memory, my right to feel this pain.

It simply comes with this ridiculous privilege of aging. This final letting go of all that is or ever will be.

I want it.

I want to live with this feeling, these thoughts, until the end as I dust out these webs that have remained here far too long now.

I am done with it.

Let me speak.

THE HOLY BIBLE
Translated by the fpecial Command of King JAMES I, of *England*

THE FIRST BOOK OF MOSES, CALLED

GENESIS

CHAPTER 3.

[16]Unto the woman he said, I will greatly multiply thy sorrow and thy conception; in sorrow thou shalt bring forth children; and thy desire shall be to thy husband, and he shall rule over thee.

December 4, 1861

Great-grandpa Zenas Jabez Condit was a zealot.

I first heard that lacerating word as it was whispered by Grandma Laura during baby cousin Lillie May Belle's christening.

Should have stayed in Pennsylvania.

I felt her sharp add-on in Grandpa Moses' ear as they sat in the pew directly behind us at First Presbyterian. Maybe she wanted us all to hear, especially Zenas.

Hhumpf, Zenas muttered loudly then followed the phlegm-starter by a cough as if he actually had something coming up his throat besides disdain.

We all knew better that this was not the place for such a moment. When he turned back to give the devil's eye that we believed him famous for, it was not Grandma Laura who was the target.

Mind your wife!

Zenas glared the words in a direct line back at Moses who ignored the eye glare.

He ain't my preacher.

Moses said this to anyone listening.

By now, I could see Mrs. Jones leaning back to hear from five pews up. Four-year-old Clara sitting next to me took my hand to still herself from the adult emotions surrounding her.

Emma was doing her best to be present then, but she provided little comfort or protection as we would later learn.

Poor cousin, Lillie May Belle. She would never know there was such an extended family stir up on her baptism day, but I would never forget the Old Testament lesson from that service.

I remember looking up at Zenas during the reading, watching him silently recite the passage, mouthing the words as it was read by an elder. His narrow, wrinkly lips moving in synch and his right fist clenched as if he were going to raise it up for emphasis. An ordained ruling elder of the Upper Ten-Mile Presbyterian. He had brought this privilege with him.

The fear of God was no match for my trembling that Sunday morning seated next to Great-grandpa Zenas.

Wild Rose (*Rosa pratincola*).

Description.—Low shrub with very prickly stem; compound leaves of 7-11 leaflets, broadly elliptical to oblong-oblanceolate, subcuneate at base, short stalked or sessile, serrate; stipule, narrow glandular toothed; flowers corymbose, calyx tube urn-shaped, 5 sepals, smooth or occasionally hispid, petals 5, rose-colored; fruit oblong, ovaries hairy.

Distribution.—Common everywhere in Iowa.

Extermination.—Thorough cultivation for a few seasons will, however, usually destroy the weed.

Rose.

For a gnarly, sharp weed some settlers called the wild prairie rose.

Emma.

For all that my mother could not or would not be.

My identity was to be such a combination of appropriate misfortune. A role cast before I had uttered a first word.

On one good day, Emma would tell me she saw the wild rose for its beauty in a terrain she otherwise detested. I do believe this was the closest she ever came to telling me that I was beautiful.

It must have been a flower she truly loved, as she and Grandma Phoebe had surrounded the Condit house with wild rose bushes shortly after Grandpa Syl had passed. Of course, Grandma Laura had chided them for replanting wild roses and not ordering cultivated ones to be shipped from back east.

Through them all, but especially Grandpa Syl, I learned that I was

smart for a girl,

pretty for a Parmlee,

hard worker like a Condit.

When Emma and Henry had married in 1850 on that same day in March that was to become my birthday many birth days later, it meant that she would be reminded of her marriage on the same day each year that Grandma Phoebe presented her glorious angel food in my honor.

My favorite.

I was so sorry about it that I had told her once so when I was 10. She had smiled with her tight, pursed lips, and briefly nodded, but continued peeling the potatoes as if I had not even spoken.

I am certain I saw the nod. That fleeting acknowledgment of understanding.

A rarity for sure.

It's just her way, Henry would tell us.

Of course your mother loves you.

Eventually, we all learned to make excuses for Emma.

□ William ○ Agnes

□ Robert

○ Elizabeth
(Mayflower)

□ Asaph

○ **Lillie May Belle**

It's sort of like that when you live in a house that someone died in. You think you might hear the voices of the former residents whispering to you.

Odd little things happen.

Pictures on the wall tilt and you know it wasn't you who did it when you last swiped them with your feather duster. A door to the sitting room suddenly squeaks ajar, yet no one is there.

Actually, it was my sister Clara who found the box and showed it to me that week. I was not surprised.

That year, Annie, Clara and I had moved into the Condit house in Parkhurst. Grandma Phoebe was gone and she had willed it to Emma, who was also gone by then, too, so Henry said it was all ours. Henry D. or H.D., Harry as we knew him, had his own home in Davenport by this time and would never have come back to Parkhurst anyway.

Go live with those river rats.

He would spat at us, and we would smile at our selfish little brother. Lillie May would smile then, too, as if she agreed with us. But truth be told, as Grandma Laura would say, she just always smiled even in tense moments.

Actually, the more tense it became, the more she smiled.

I had watched out of the corner of my eye as I poured coffee

---

for the kindly census worker when he wrote *head of household* under my name on the census card. You can only imagine my smile then.

If only Emma could have seen it. Of course, I made sure that Harry knew it was put into the 1910 record. He had mumbled something about the chronic errors of civil workers.

It's my job to keep us three sisters together.

Spinsters' row they had begun to call our church pew at First Presbyterian. Three unwed sisters and Widow Jones's regular Sunday morning seats. I was informally charged to ensure that nothing happened to any of us. If only the good Lord could bestow such a power, but I do most certainly serve as spokeswoman.

I do not even feel old, yet the title remained stuck.

At this age, and when marriage was no longer an option, there is no other title left for women like me. I do not blame them.

Yet, my life and my family's houses were still full of surprises.

As Clara held up the box for both of us to see, I glimpsed the corner of what looked like folded pages beneath the 1904 drugstore calendar with the months still all intact behind tiny staple pins that held them so delicately in place below a New Year's cherub atop Old Man Time.

The note that covered the delicate, almost sheer, pages did not hide the inkwell blurred writing that melted through to each page. I picked up a black and white photo of a woman about my age standing on what must have been the riverside porch to the Condit house. I could see she was gazing out to the river that still ran in front of the house and I turned the picture over to read 1864.

She had lost only two children by then. The river was certainly still here, so it must have been what she had been looking at.

You did not look at the camera in those days.

Underneath the photo were the missing pages from the Sargent family Bible and a yellowed clipping from *The New York Times*.

The Bible pages were worn very thin and would crumble if I didn't ever so delicately turn to the last page of the Tilley branch of the family tree, which was a page all its own, almost a full tree of its own.

Siblings?

Someone had penciled in charcoal, and then had erased, in the margin next to Agnes (Tylle) and William Tilley's wedding date.

Erased, but still visible.

PARKHURST. All the pioneer laws of a new country were enforced here, and that same rigid regard for the rights of all was duly noticed. Some very rough specimens of humanity were of course among the early settlers, and many a kind heart covered up a very rough exterior. It was deemed, in those days, a very dangerous thing for one man to jump another's claim. The man who had the temerity to attempt such a thing was looked upon as likely to do worse deeds when opportunity presented.

The great river has an unexpected symmetry this morning.

It rallies against itself like a current so stuck in its own swirling that it creates pockets of captured movement as if pausing to consider me like a portrait photographer, waiting for me to join in.

Yet, somehow I know you won't take me with you today.

Sadness comes through me this morning and like the river's bold current, it washes me clean, taking me to that next beckoning passage.

Fortunately, these moments do not stay with me as they did in the old days. Now, they simply pass on by more like the slightest lap against bank rock and then gone. Or like the carp that tips its nose just above the surface and then a flip and a flap, it's gone, too.

If you are not looking, you missed it. You missed out.

I am curious now with no pain.

Perhaps I simply slip away beneath the water.

Unnoticed.

Missed out.

Forgotten.

First, I must be clear regarding all of this debris that can become tangled in this passing and caught up along the way like Grandpa Syl's fishing line.

Cut bait.

He would tell me this with all of his faux sternness, a façade that overlay his kind heart. There was no actual scolding when I did not understand.

Here, let me show you.

The patient teacher I could never have been. An Iowa dirt farmer by choice who came at each day as if it were still his first day crossing the river and soon to be his last. Only too grateful for having set foot on the other side.

If only I could have lived like that.

What a morning.

He would almost shout this out to the dawn rather than Grandma Phoebe. He was the best in me. It is not just now that I can see this.

I am pleased with myself today that no dark woman stands over me this morning, berating like she would in the old days, scolding me when no light could be seen or felt in this tunnel I awoke to last week.

Dying is not an efficient task.

Let's get on with the living, as Syl would have said, or what's the use.

Yet, I am finding that the coming to terms is not more difficult than burying your baby brother, or your own mother, or your

best sister because here you can detach somehow. Life sometimes lets you do just that, so consider yourself as better off. In
your life, the lights will simply go out.

My life has been full as it could get. No room for more.

John Forrest never had the privilege of getting on with it. Better
off, they all had said, but they never saw me hold that tiny body
in my own childish hands and willing him to eat.

He is happier now that he found the Lord so quickly.

Acceptance was a beautiful gift—its beauty taught to me by
grandparents who had lost much more than they had gained by
the end.

I had used as much as I could of what I had learned from them. I
had always done my best to see to that. One regret that I do not
have to suffer from now.

Walk the talk.

I hope they would have been proud of me.

When it is your own soul that must move on to find your way
through all of this aloneness, there can be a blessing in the
indifference. That is until you awake one night to find your sis-
ter-in-law at your bedside with the needle.

I still call it our house, although Harry and Lillie May have long
since taken over the rest of it. Now I feel like a visitor when I
make the rare trip to the downstairs. I feel better when I think
of it as Grandpa's house. The house that Grandpa Syl died in
that afternoon he had pounded the final nail into the doorframe.

Although my keepers have decided that this house is already
theirs, even though I am still clearly breathing upstairs, nothing

can keep me from this bedroom with a spectacular view of all that I need. At least they have that much sympathy for me and know well that I was once the head of this household back when my sisters were alive and we cared for father here after Emma had passed.

When I am ready, this river will carry me home, the same as it did for her. For all of them.

It comforts me now to think like that.

It's really all that I have left.

The Domesday Book

or the Great Survey of England of William the Conquerer
XXXII. The land of Walter the Fleming
[Folio 215V: Bedfordshire]

In Henlow Hugh holds 3½ hides of Walter. There is land for 3½ ploughs. In demesne [is] 1 plough, and there can be another. There are 4 villans with 2 ploughs, and 4 bordars and 2 flaves, meadow for 3½ ploughs, and 1 mill render 34S. All together it is worth 60S; when received 40S; TRE 70S. 6 fokemen held this land and they could give their land to whom they wished.

1543, Henlow Parish, Bedfordshire

Bachelor and Spinster.

William and Agnes's official pre-marital statuses were registered in the Henlow parish record when they went to see the vicar for their license to wed.

When your king does as he pleases, thumbs his nose at the pope, and declares himself divine, one can only imagine the impact this must have had upon the small parish of Henlow. To hear of the beheadings at Tower Hill kept the community of Henlow quite secretive over the years as to their own opinions of the crown and the goings on of the current sovereign.

Quietly they lived as they always had, whispering their complaints in a small circle around the sloshed pub table, well out of earshot of the vicar outside St. Mary's vestibule. Even the notables were somewhat afraid, although it certainly did not slow their egoist boasting over their own parish achievements.

So, there was no specific cause for inquiry when a Tilley married a Tylle.

It happened then and still does in England and here for that matter.

Cousins often married cousins.

The vicar had only wrongly thought that William and Agnes were brother and sister. After all, had he not performed their first communion himself, four years apart?

So it was their mother who accompanied them to register their desire to wed, to set the record straight, to clarify. Since the parish was as willing to accept the tariff for the most ridiculous of matrimonies, she knew it would not take long.

A sovereign would be paid, so no banns would be posted.

You are mistaken.

Mother Margaret had so convincingly feigned the union. Agnes is the daughter of my poor, dear sister, you see, who lost her way with the inquisitors. Tied to the rack she was. Yes, ghastly.

I could not let her baby girl see her pain nor take on such shame, now could I?

I took her in as my own.

Cousins, you see.

Tylle is my family.

Shamed by my sister, yes a witch! So ashamed to say it aloud, I can only whisper the word.

Agnes had never witnessed her mother speak so swiftly or so sure. How dare she be so forward with the vicar?

Cousins! Betrothed since she was seven!

Some in Henlow said the last name was Tilley and some will always claim Tylle. Not uncommon in a day when daughters took their mother's maiden, sons their father's. See, it was all within God's plan. An appropriate marriage for sure, an affinity preserved.

'Tis our land, not loanland for sure. The lord hath said it in do-

mesday and would say it as sure today!

By the time the crown had set forth the canons to redeem itself from the sins of the former, the Tilley-Tylle union had celebrated its 20th year, birthed four healthy children, only one a son, and a family remained resolved that their venture to see to it that all of their property was protected had been tremendous fortune.

It was family, just and right.

No foolish, hedonist king claiming to be godly or his bastard daughter would take from them what was theirs since the Saxons. They had worked much too hard to see it dowered away.

> *No person shall marry within the degrees prohibited by the laws of God, and expressed in a table set forth by authority in the year of our Lord God 1563. And all marriages so made and contracted shall be adjudged incestuous and unlawful, and consequently dissolved from the beginning…*

Agnes would never come to read the Crown's canon. Of course, she would never learn to read. In her 59th year, her own son had to read her husband's will to her. But, oh she had been so proud that day of her vital betroth, as her father had called it.

So adamant he had been.

That day when he had paid so close attention to his daughter. The day she had saved the family as he so loudly proclaimed, beaming at her so violently.

The day he had believed in her enough to teach Agnes Tylle to sign her own name!

AN ACT
to Divide the Territory of Wisconsin and to establish the Territorial Government of Iowa

Be it enacted by the Senate and House of Representatives of the United States of America in Congress assembled, That from and after the third day of July next, all that part of the present Territory of Wisconsin which lies west of the Mississippi to the Territorial line, shall, for the purposes of temporary Government, be and constitute a separate Territorial Government by the name of Iowa.

APPROVED JUNE 12, 1838

The sun set in the east today.

This reversal was how it appeared to me as the river reflected the setting sun into my east window.

Reflection.

A mirror of light to beauty.

Perhaps the reflection is showing me one last time.

Harry tells me not to talk like that when he brings me my pills this morning, but I know they count the days now, and I am guilty of doing the same.

My Anna Viola's name was not even properly engraved on the family mausoleum. At least in death someone might have paid some respect. But, 30 years prior, Henry had told the engraver that her name was Annie V., as that is what he had always called her. Why would he not rethink it for perpetuity? And who was to listen to me back then to correct it after he was gone?

He was the one who had called us Rosie and Annie. For many years, he was the only one.

It was likely my last outing today.

One knows these things when we are in our final days. Harry and Lillie May kindly drove me to our mausoleum at Pine Hill to pay respects to our family and so that I could see that my name had been engraved as I wished.

Of course it was stated only as Rose E., as if the engraver had run out of room for my second name, that eternal brand of my mother that I would not escape even at death.

E.

Like a branding for life on a soul that had no idea what it was to carry it forward.

Of course, I had been relieved when Emma died. I can say this only now as I write these words here without fear of retribution, recrimination, her silent rebuke.

My words matter here.

For far too long they resided only in my mind, repeated only to myself, shared in silence.

Such a very loud silence!

If I have held these thoughts to myself for these 90 years, only she knew what it was to carry such grief in this resounding silence from which we came to know from her. We left her in the protective circle that silence can offer when you own no other boundaries.

I can still picture that stoic face: jaw set as if haughtiness were in her nature. But any elitism was a very false perception of Emma. Today, I like to believe I can finally forgive her rather than pity her.

Pity can be so self-righteous.

Annie would tell me I was so cold-hearted when I would say that I never felt any warmth from Emma, but I was really not saying it to be cruel or selfish. Perhaps my brother Harry felt some warmth. He seemed to be the only one of us she ever let close.

Piqued, drawn Harry. Her only son who had lived.

Propping myself up to balance on my cane as the third leg of this old stool, I traced my hand down the list of names on the east side of the mausoleum this afternoon.

I tried to touch, to remember Emma's grief, the reason for her distance from me. From us all.

I had to stop then. Take a breath. Look again.

I knew this story too well. And its aftermath.

That's what they used to call the four of us who had lived.

The second family.

Thunder Clan

□———— Mukataquet ————

□———— Nanamakee ————

□———— Paisa Pyesa ————

□—— "Black Hawk" ——
Makataimeshekiakiak

□—— **"Whirling Thunder"** ——
Seuskuk

August 2, 1832, Victory, Wisconsin

Some still claim Black Hawk's son survived that last battle at Bad Axe, the last ambush planned to rid the Sac from this great riverfront someone later named River Road.

Once and for all.

Retreat.

Removal.

Exclusion.

Nasheaskuk had pressed himself into that dry bluff dirt, angled amid billion-year-old protrusions arched with toes that hung on, panting to live out that sweltering dog day as he peered down to see his sisters bloodied, and one floating just below him at water's edge like a bloated muskrat trapped in its own shore fortress.

He turned away then.

He had the sight even from this distance as his grandfather had always told him he would.

You will outlive them all.

Pyesa had declared it. When you do, he had warned, you must remember never to bow before those that imitate our thunder. Their sticks and drums only mimic the source of here and hereafter. Yours is from the deeper source.

You are whirling thunder.

Do not respect their power as it is fired by a great fear. Hatred has much fury at its outset, but it will always eventually turn back on itself. He had said the words as if carving them into his skin. It felt that hard and painful.

He was very young and did not really ever understand the meaning until now when his toes were aching and he admired even his own persistence to hang on.

The test is patience, his grandfather had always reminded him. He used that now and it was working. It gave him something other than what he saw and heard below.

Nasheaskuk could hear those words as if his grandfather was behind him, whispering with that rolling depth he used for the most important of messages. But it was overpowered by a softer, low murmur of his grandmother. Her lower octaves always underscored his grandfather's loud clap of words. Together their force lifted him and now he adamantly kept those toes encamped on a blistering hot rock as if he were a volunteer tree rising perpendicular to the bluff.

A solid young tree, strong enough to bend with whatever came at him. He would not break.

Grandmother took his hand and he felt it, but no tears could fall now. He was a warrior and had turned his heart off and emotion would have to come later, only after this white man's harangue with guns not words. She, too, would not have cried for the mother and her children, a slaughter of people for their secrets, but would have stood with him and prayed for their spirits to quickly depart so as to not feel the pain of this ugly cowardice. An ambush by those who could not understand their own stance.

They continued to fire with their false-thunder, an embarrassing impersonation of the power of the great river spirit, our great mother of waters who loved us all as only his grandmother had taught him. He clearly heard her say this and so his toes remained in place till it was over.

It had been all that saved him that day.

Nasheaskuk stood in line with others who had survived that last battle along with those that had never resisted the new great father as they said goodbye to the Mesquakie. Chained at the wrists and ankles as if he were owned now by something other than himself.

All who had been forced to cross the great river, camped along the soon-to-be Parkhurst where Eleazer had arrived, and then pushed on again, and again, eventually to Stroud where Mary and the others would be born.

It was the thunder calling us home; Black Hawk had told him when he decided to not follow his people to Oklahoma.

The real thunder.

I will follow you soon enough, he had told him before they had bound his legs in the chains. He called out from the line of warriors that stood with him.

Quiet.

A guard had called out to him, but Black Hawk kept up his words.

Whirling Thunder, you must lead them now. We remain proud as our pride is never lost. As they pushed him away, he said one final word as if it came straight from Peya.

Remember.

Do not hang your head as we are Thunder Clan, rolling our presence louder than the new great father who faces a false mirror each morning, seeing himself as the source of all—believing his false wisdom will change the world order.

Retribution is never for free.

False acts and orders cannot control forever. This mirror is made of glass and will one day shatter into the shards of his deeds. Shards that will one day seek his own blood for what he has done.

He does not replace Great Father. Will never be.

Remember now that the stars will blanket your sleep the same as they do right here. It was what Black Hawk had shared in his last good-night before the slaughter as he and his eldest son had turned to watch their very last moon rise over the great river.

His father had no idea what he had done.

Fifth General Assembly of the State of Iowa

SECTION 1. *Be it enacted by the General Assembly of the State of Iowa,* That the consent of the State is hereby given that the Indians now residing in Tama county known as a portion of the Sacs and Foxes, be permitted to remain and reside in said State, and that the Governor be requested to inform the Secretary of War thereof, and urge on said department, the propriety of paying said Indians their proportion of the annuities due or to become due to said Tribe of Sacs and Fox Indians.

APPROVED JUNE 15TH, 1856

So it goes with family secrets.

You think they are buried or that somehow time has erased them. In our family we liked to say that some people would take secrets to their grave. We liked to believe that once all the carriers of the skeletons were dead, there was no one left to tell.

But secrets are really more like the mudpuppies, the great river bottom feeders.

They live unsuspected, unassuming in the deepest, darkest waters of the great river, but eventually they are caught and brought up to the light. I have come to learn that more energy is put into keeping the secret from the light than was ever put into examining them in full view. My family has been no exception.

Too painful, some might say.

Too hard, they wouldn't say.

Courage? I don't think so.

Yet, I have learned that family secrets are viciously motivating, even transcendent over space and time, generations and countries, oceans and rivers.

But once a mudpuppy appears, having fed for years on the larvae and waste of the river bottom, it undergoes a metamorphosis.

The secret is dissected by the light.

When my sister Annie and I were young, we liked to believe we could keep each other's secrets. But we learned soon enough that secrets are never really kept. We liked to believe that we were the guardians of a sisterly trust; *never, ever, swear on the Bible, spit thrice, never betray my sister.*

But even if a secret is never shared aloud, it exists within the secretkeeper.

Like the 100-year-old catfish at the bottom of the river, secrets are eventually caught and brought to surface to be examined for all of their oddities and comforting homeliness. Yet, the longer they thrive at the river bottom, they need continued care and feeding as they grow and grow and grow.

I once saw an 80-pound catfish on the front page of the *Davenport Gazette*. It was the ugliest-looking fish, almost prehistoric. The aged being had been brought up, brought to surface and exposed to the sunlight off the fisherman's pier down on the levee by the green tree. Exposed so that all of us could view the wonder of its lack of spectacularity,

its peculiarities,

its ugliness.

An ugly beauty.

It's like that with secrets.

Along with the entire horror aura when brought into the light, we can't help ourselves from looking. We have to look.

We are taken in by horror.

It's like trying to squelch a laugh in church; it finds its way out. Joy can be like that; so can secrets.

So if we are not afraid to steal that peek at what we may perceive is ugly, we might, just might, be able to see the glimmer, the gleam of something beautiful.

The Ancestor

John Cunditt
_____
Wales

Jabez Condit
_____
New Jersey

Zenas
_____
Pennsylvania

Sylvester
_____
Iowa

September 4, 1862

Jesus was a carpenter.

That was the first thing Zenas said to me when he had met all four of us children at Grandpa Syl's the day after he arrived from back east.

I seemed to already know his story as if it were written down somewhere.

Zenas had learned his first vocation as a carpenter's apprentice and saved enough money to acquire 400 acres between Greene and Washington Counties. Left with his eldest son, Ira, who had stayed there to follow Syl to Iowa for his last days.

He was named Zenas Jabez for the sons of Philip Condit son of Peter Condit, son of John Cunditt, the ancestor.

Blue-blood, Grandpa had always said under his breath when Grandma Laura had said too much about her heritage.

I did not understand the difference back then.

Rosie, your last name may be Parmlee, but you are a Condit who can actually name your ancestors.

Ask Moses if he can do that, Grandpa Syl would say to me, but he was not really saying it to me.

Zenas Jabez carried the name of his father, Jabez Condit of Prosperity, Pennsylvania, a town named for the wishes and prayers of its founders and a petulant contrition.

There was nothing more American than Washington County. Named for none other than the first president it had been, Grandpa Syl told me when I was five. Memorize all of them, he had said, and recite them in order when you can prove it. Assignment given and delivered before I turned six. He knew I was bright; he told me so when I had completed my presidential recitation. Especially for a girl, he always added.

Zenas wasn't quite as generous with his compliments, though he was not with us long by the time he arrived in Iowa. All of the Condits back east feared liturgical debate with him, Grandpa Syl had explained to me without pride.

I could not imagine how Zenas had ever been a father to anyone.

Fanatic.

Even at 81, he would puff his chest and stand up straighter as if it were a badge of honor. That and the fathering of his 8 sons (5 daughters) were enough to satisfy his entry into heaven.

Grandpa Syl was the second son, which I always guessed was how it was us who ended up with Zenas in those final days and his brother ended up with the farm.

Who else would take such abuse and still bathe the old man?

At least he never saddled me with that name.

I overheard him tell this to Grandma Phoebe as they readied the house for the viewing.

I would never meet my Pennsylvania cousins. Too far, they had all said, to come for the funeral.

Iowa Code 1954

595.19 Void Marriages.

1. Marriages between the following persons who are related by blood are void:

    a. Between a man and his father's sister, mother's sister, daughter, sister, son's daughter, daughter's daughter, brother's daughter, or sister's daughter.

    b. Between a woman and her father's brother, mother's brother, son, brother, son's son, daughter's son, brother's son, or sister's son.

    c. Between first cousins.

2. Marriages between persons either of whom has a husband or wife living are void, but, if the parties live and cohabit together after the death or divorce of the former husband or wife, such marriage shall be valid.

I would be fourteen years old before I ever found a solitary moment to be alone again with the Sargent family Bible. There was
no Parmlee family Bible to be found anywhere.

No names.

No legacy.

No history there. Only the one we would make for ourselves in
Iowa was what Grandpa Moses had always said. Crossing the
river gave that privilege, I guessed.

What we had was our Treat heritage. Even as a teenage girl, I
could not understand how Moses had persuaded Grandma Laura to come with him to the new territory.

She was of *the* New England Treats, founders of Watertown and
Glastonbury. Advocates for the purest of religions and education
of the *new* England in Connecticut.

A fine New England family with the cleanest of lines back to
England.

Grandma Laura told me often of the stories of great-great-
great grandpa Treat, the Reverend who went to Yale, whose
great-grandfather, another Reverend Treat, actually knew John
Harvard!

That's why you are such a good reader, Rose, you get it from my
side of the family, she would proudly declare, staking claim to

part of me as her own.

No family Bible was needed for me to explore her family tree. Her tapestries openly told her lineage and ours the few times she let me take a look, but never on my own. She was right by my side turning the fragile pages herself, pointing out the names as if it were the Tudor genealogy on English parchment.

Each time she would share the Treat stories, out would come the carefully wrapped, delicate parcels pressed in the center pages of an immense Bible.

At the bottom, she had always stitched the same quote

In the soft scenes of life when cares are small and few I show to others of my age what busy hands can do.

L.A.T, 1805

Miss Anna Cornwall's School for Girls

The United States of America, To all to whom these Presents shall come, Greeting:

Whereas Sylvester G. Condit of Scott County, Iowa Territory has deposited in the General Land Office of the United States, a Certificate of the Register of the Land Office at Du Buque whereby it appears that full payment has been made by the said Sylvester G. Condit according to the provisions of the Act of Congress of the 24th of April, 1820, entitled An Act making further provision for the sale of the Public Lands, for the South East quarter of Section five, in Township seventy eight, North of Range five, East of the fifth Principal Meridian, in the District of Lands subject to sale at Du Buque, Iowa Territory, containing one hundred and sixty acres.

Tenth day of November
in the Year of our Lord one thousand eight hundred and forty-one
and of the Independence of the United States the sixty-sixth

May 25, 1881

Grandpa Syl had hammered that last nail in the house on River Road on a Thursday morning and they had begun to move in.

By Thursday afternoon, Grandpa Syl was dead.

Fortunately it was May, so he was in the ground by Saturday morning. As I stood at the carefully dug grave site atop the hill that we used to call pioneer cemetery, but would later be named Parkhurst Cemetery as more and more Condits and Sargents would find eternal rest there, but not the Parmlees, I swore I heard him call for me.

RoseEmma.

By then, Emma had so many of her own ghosts, that I could not share this startling event with her. But I distinctly heard Grandpa Syl call out my name as he always had when he could not find me. Saying it as if it were all one name.

RoseEmma.

It was only then that I had cried.

Grandma Phoebe had some money after Grandpa Syl died.

She had no idea of his monetary worth when he was alive, but his attorney had seen to explain it to her. It was almost acceptable for a widow to own property and even wealth in 1881.

The money drew suitors and speculators and looks she would

simply disregard at the ladies aid. Privately, she enjoyed a great humor over this. Think what Syl would say now, she would say and laugh and laugh. She was more beautiful when she laughed, even though she never thought so.

It would be weeks after the funeral before I could again visit Aunt Mary-Ann and find alone time with the Sargent Bible.

But, of course, weeks become months become years.

Back here! I had yelled, carefully closing the doors on the Bible stand.

Where's Mary-Ann? Grandpa Syl had asked.

She took Lillie May and went to check on Mrs. Parkhurst, I replied.

Just finished hammering the last nail in the new house! he gleamed through a grin like I had never seen on him.

Let's go find Grandma and celebrate.

We're moving in!

THE EMIGRANT'S GUIDE

A Glimpse of Iowa.

Scott County

This is one of the river counties, situated north of Muscatine, and occupying nearly a central position in the Territory, from north to south; there being four counties below and four above, bordering upon the Mississippi. Ever since the earliest settlement of Iowa, this portion has been justly esteemed among the most desirable and fascinating regions of the boundless West. Being entirely free from low bottom lands, (the usual causes of disease,) it was early selected by the sagacious pioneers, among the favored spots of the upper Mississippi valley.

Even after 90 years of this view, the thought of never seeing this river again is almost as painful as the thought of giving up breathing.

At the close of each day, I look out over the ever-moving sur-face and picture her on the river porch as the sun would set in a pink and lavender haze behind the one and one-half story wood frame, her faded gray skirt's frayed edges tipping the tops of her high-buttoned black hard leather shoes that mangled bone and cartilage, molding wide feet to narrow and aching against the day, contrasted against a soft palette of subdued rose light, softer than that of the orange and red gloriousness that arose over the river each morning and gave her no solace but a brilliant call to start each day as if every day were Easter morning.

Rather, it was only in that soft, end-of-day light that Emma let her emotions she had carried throughout another long day emerge briefly. As short as an exhale, the sun's decline allowed her to lower the resistance that she held intact till it began to set.

Taking in the sunset gave her a peace that may have been the only peace she felt in a world where she believed that being on guard was her female duty, her obligation to herself, her own assemblage of protective structures.

Only a weakness of heart, a weakness of birth could understand why she kept it all so hidden.

At least in this act of self-protection, she had done her day's penance and as she looked at the back of her hands as she raised them to align with the colors of the sky, she felt strength in her own ability to keep everyone out, since dying was not an option until the dear Lord told her it was time to come home.

No one can understand what it was like when you crossed the river unless you had, Emma had always said.

Everyone became your family then.

SKETCHES OF IOWA,

OR THE

EMIGRANT'S GUIDE;

CONTAINING

A CORRECT A CORRECT DESCRIPTION OF THE AGRICULTURAL AND
MINERAL RESOURCES, GEOLOGICAL FEATURES AND STATISTICS OF THE
TERRITORY OF IOWA,

A MINUTE DESCRIPTION OF EACH COUNTY, AND OF THE
PRINCIPAL TOWNS AND INDIAN VILLAGES,

PRAIRIE AND TIMBERED LANDS,

A VIEW OF THE RAPID INCREASE AND FUTURE PROSPECTS
OF THE PEOPLE, MORAL AND PHYSICAL,

Traits of Indian Character,

WITH SKETCHES OF

BLACK HAWK, AND OTHERS:

BEING THE RESULT OF MUCH OBSERVATION AND TRAVEL DURING A
CONTINUOUS RESIDENCE OF SERVERAL YEARS

BY JOHN B. NEWHALL,
BURLINGTON, IOWA.

"The West—the West—on every breeze
Is borne an echo from the West."

PUBLISHED BY J. H. COLTON,
MERCHANTS' EXCHANGE,
New-York

1841.

March 2, 1833

Emma clutched Amelia, hugging her porcelain head so tightly as she took her almost-three-year-old steps across the expanse of ice, so wide, so cold.

Phoebe was far ahead with the baby in her arms. Above her, she could see the outline of their guide's bull straw hat at the front of the line, reminding them of the spring to come and where they were headed. So tall and lanky was the guide that Emma could see him even from her position as last in line.

Heaviest folks in front!

The guide had yelled, a false confidence it likely was, but they so wanted to believe he was genuine.

Grandpa Syl kept his fears to himself.

No one should have been crossing the ice once the open waters had begun to break up.

Huge ice chunks floating through the rapids near them.

The old Red Bird had told the guide that the island canal was the last of the ice to break. At 12 to 18 inches deep, even a heavy load was safe, she had said. He believed her still.

Thank god we left that wagon in Illinois.

Hired to cross this chasm to redemption, a new life awaiting, and if he sank any settlers, he would have to go back and beg shop work from that Illinois plow maker and his grandiose delusions.

He quickly broke his own rule when he heard the cracking begin and Phoebe gave a look back to Emma, a good-bye look that she would never forget. Emma was running now, almost with a little skip so that she did not slip on the ice.

Jack be nimble. Jack be quick.

A widening crack in front of her appeared as a wide cavern ready to devour her and separate her forever from Phoebe, Syl, little sister Mary-Ann, baby John.

Emma would not be left behind them!

Come Lord Jesus, let's be blessed.

1-2-3-4

Jack jumped over the candlestick.

She kept skipping in place as the crack widened in front of her and she knew she would never skip, much less step, over this widening expansion that may as well have been the entire river for how it seemed to Emma. Water began to bubble up over the ice, turning it all to slush, soon ankle deep and freezing her ribbon-tied shoes.

Crossing this river would forever overwhelm her.

The great river they had bragged on all night at the fire. The river would now swallow her up, never allowing her to touch the shore of this new place that she could see as firm ground just ahead of her family. She had been left behind.

The rough gloved hands slid neatly under her little arms as she watched the porcelain head of her Amelia fall away, forgotten.

Amelia would take her place. She did not yet know that one day she would prefer to have been Amelia.

From atop the head of this giant, whose long strides carried her over the widening crack her short legs could not, she kept her eyes toward the tallest oak on shore.

You broke the rule, Emma whispered into the guide's ear.

I sure did.

Emma found the courage to steal a peek above his bull hat brim to see the rest of her family already climbing up the short bank.

Did she cry it aloud? She could never remember.

I want to go home.

But there was no going back now.

Up the bank they climbed.

10TH MOON, SAUKENUK

The changes of many summers have brought old age upon me, and I cannot expect to survive many moons. Before I set out on my journey to the land of my fathers, I have determined to give my motives and reasons for my former hostilities to the whites, and to vindicate my character from misrepresentation. The kindness I received from you whilst a prisoner of war assures me that you will vouch for the facts contained in my narrative, so far as they came under your observation.

I am now an obscure member of a nation that formerly honored and respected my opinions. The pathway to glory is rough, and many gloomy hours obscure it. May the Great Spirit shed light on yours, and that you may never experience the humility that the power of the American government has reduced me to, is the wish of him, who, in his native forests, was once as proud and bold as yourself.

AUTOBIOGRAPHY OF MA-KA-TAI-ME-SHE-KIA-KIAK,
BLACK HAWK;
Embracing the traditions of his nation, various wars in which he has been engaged, and his account of the cause and general history of the Black Hawk War of 1832, His Surrender, and Travels Through the United States. Dictated by Himself.

The great river was not a boundary, but a convergence.

Its watershed became an early American washbasin that cleansed the past from all who moved through it from east to west, marking their passage by the number of times they had crossed it. For my family, it was one.

Fewer ventured east than west.

The river has its myriad of tributaries, but it is eventually a higher union merges as one stream to one even greater ocean.

When one is less busy looking forward, time exists to look back. To see that it really all is not as separate as it seemed. It does eventually flow into a larger shared basin washing us all clean from our separateness, our divisions.

No one owns the ocean.

It is more difficult to notice until later in life when the adventurer has finally settled on land in one place or another.

Staked a claim.

Broke ground.

Only in these final hours does one have the time to reflect on whence they have come and where they have arrived.

Sometimes they realize all they wanted to do was get there so they could place that rocker on that porch facing back east. Many wear out a fine rocker looking back east over that trail, turning over and over the moments the crucial choices were made that led to them to here and now.

It's like that on these full moon nights when it is just the river and me. Alone with this shimmering black-navy silk carpet, a living current that has kept me company for all these years. Its movement a constant reminder of the undercurrent that lay beneath.

It knows I need my regrets, especially now. I like to think that I had choices and I made the best of them.

It may be all I really had.

In Ye Name of God, Amen.

We whofe names are underwritten, the loyal fubjects of our dead fovereigne Lord, King James, by ye grade of God, of Great Britaines, France and Ireland, King, defender of ye faith, etc. haveing undertaken for ye glory of God and advancement of ye Chriftian faith, and honour of our King and countrie, a voyage to plant ye firft Colnie in ye Northerne parts of Virginia, do by the fe prefents folumnly, and mutaly, in ye pre fence of God, and of one another, covenant and combine our felves togeather into a civil body politik for our better ordering and prefervation and furtherance of ye end afore faid, and by vertue hearof to enacte, conftitute and frame fuch juft and equal laws, ordinances, acts, conftitutions, and offices from time to time, as fhall be thought moft meete and convenient for ye generall good of ye Colonie, unto which we promife all due fubmiffion and obedience. In witnes whereof we have hereunder fubfcribed our names at Cape-Codd ye 11 of November in ye year of ye raigne of our fovereigne Lord, King James of England, France and Ireland, ye eighteenth, and of Scotland ye fiftie-fourth Ano Dom. 1620.

1. John Carver,
2. William Bradford,
3. Mr Edward Winslow,
4. William Brewster.
5. Isaac Allerton,
6. Myles Standish,
7. John Alden,
8. John Turner,
9. Francis Eaton,
10. James Chilton,
11. John Craxton,
12. John Billington,
13. Moses Fletcher,
14. John Goodman,
15. Samuel Fuller,
16. Christopher Martin,
17. William Mullins,
18. William White,
19. Richard Warren,
20. John Howland,
21. Steven Hopkins,
22. Digery Priest,
23. Thomas Williams,
24. Gilbert Winslow,
25. Edmund Margesson,
26. Peter Brown,
27. Richard Britteridge
28. George Soule,
29. Edward Tilly,
30. John Tilly,
31. Francis Cooke,
32. Thomas Rogers,
33. Thomas Tinker,
34. John Ridgdale
35. Edward Fuller,
36. Richard Clark,
37. Richard Gardiner,
38. John Allerton,
39. Thomas English,
40. Edward Doten,
41. Edward Liester.

Sometimes marriage comes out of necessity over false notions of love and romance.

I am certainly no expert, but I came to understand this at such an early age and it was something I could never speak of as no one wants to hear about the challenges of marriage from one who has never succumbed. Or one who was never chosen, as Lillie liked to barb. I like to think of it more as a choice, one of my own choosing.

Thank goodness your brother carried on the line and your father would be proud of that.

She would say as she tucked the loose sheets around me with the gossipy tone of a hotel maid cleaning up after uncouth guests. I was still there to listen to her bites that cut as deeply as if she stood over me with Grandma Phoebe's butcher knife newly razored, carving out legs and wings.

Everyone forgave Lillie no matter what words departed those sweet lips. We had done it for so long; there was no changing it now. Women can be so cruel to women.

Our connection was simple.

Puritans arrived. Natives were purged.

It was all right and good to be on the side of the European.

John Howland had hitched a ride on the Mayflower as a servant and came out as a leader to claim one Elizabeth Tilley.

Safety. Union.

Matrimony. Survival.

We all became cousins then.

□——Sylvester——○——Phoebe——

○——Mary-Ann——   ○——Emma——

○——**Lillie Mae Belle**——□——**H. D.**——

The day of Harry and Lillie May's wedding was like the great river convergence.

The great river watershed converged into one channel, one course, an assimilation of Treats-Sargents-Parmlees and Condits that would forever be joined as a legacy, property, lineage.

No one talked about the blood problems in 1907. After all, the queen herself had married her own first cousin, the prince.

It was exclusiveness, a protection of sorts. Much like the royals, it kept our family within its own inner circle.

Protected.

These were like the meandering tributaries that eventually had wandered so far off the original stream they had cut themselves off from their original source.

Banded and cautered.

A flame so hot that no memory of pain had even registered.

By 1954, Harry and Lillie May were still happily married with three healthy children, so a simple matter of blood did not even ever arise as a concern. It was probably more of an oddity for their descendants to consider than it was for me by then.

Yet, Henry and Emma had both feared the spark they saw between these two children who were raised practically as siblings.

Though Lillie was the elder, Harry acted with a heavy hand over Lillie May's speech and manner even from a very young age.

Mary-Ann and Asaph were even less enthusiastic about the alliance, which came as a surprise to me.

I had expected their worldview to be a bit broader than Emma's who I had expected to be the one to put her foot down against such a union. Yet, I suppose it was just another one of her ways to keep Harry happy, to muster whatever happiness could be offered in this world she seemed to detest.

At least with Lillie May, he had kept it all in the family.

No other devil in-laws to deal with that he did not already know well.

No family dramas to bear beyond those he already had survived.

No dark-sided personas to emerge than the shadows than those he already lived with. Harry's sensibilities likely preferred such a setting for matrimony.

Besides, the Sargents *had all that land!*

Harry would never be a dirt farmer from Iowa. He would own the dirt, but someone else would get their hands dirty. The future father of his children, his empire to be built from the work of those who came before.

No, Mary-Ann and Asaph looked less fondly on the possibility of their only daughter taking up with her entrusted nephew taking her hand as his wife. You can only imagine the talk at the ladies society. I don't know how my sisters and I sat through it.

At first, both their parents could not bear it.

Yet, at the end of the day, Lillie May loved Harry and she always had. It may have been a mixed-up kind of sibling-like, cousin love at first, but then it grew into something more permanent.

Then needed.

She needed it for always and finally her mother saw that simple truth. Lillie May was not strong like Mary. She needed a man, so it may as well have been our Harry.

After all, Lillie had been telling the family since she was eight years old that she loved her cousin. We would smile and then benignly gasp as if it were a shocking surprise, believing then such immature proclamations would never survive adolescence.

Perhaps if Grandma Laura were still around it would have never been allowed. She was probably the only one of us who had the strength to say no.

Don't be foolish.

But without her input, Emma never connected any wrongness to this budding relationship. She just went on with that tilt to her head and stoicism paid for in those long nights on prairie grass beds before any house was built, when a fire circle chat dispelled the dark fear of natives and coyote.

Survival.

Necessary partnerships for the breath of life.

So it was to be. Harry's aunt became his mother-in-law; Lillie May's aunt Emma was gone seven years before, so she would never know our Emma as hers. She would only remember the stony aunt she barely knew, the one that the grandmother they shared made excuses for as the one her own mother, Emma's sister, could not understand.

Henry had died that same year, so the only permission to be gained was from Asaph and Mary-Ann who were more concerned by that time about titles and deed transfers than their own daughter.

I looked over at the father of the bride (uncle of the groom) and wondered to myself whether 11 fingers and 11 toes had crossed his mind. Mary-Ann likely. The bride and groom likely did not know nor cared that they shared a Treat great-great grandfather on both branches of the same family tree.

The only relatives who would condemn this union were long ago in the ground. If naysayers were here, they did not make their presence known to the groom, who showed little discomfort or nervousness. His church-face piety already in full use.

My sisters and I took our regular pew with no pretense or any confusion on which side of the church to be seated. We had come to watch this lottery of homesteads for we had to see it for ourselves as much as we were obligated to attend as sisters of the groom and first cousins of the bride.

Land offices in Dubuque and Iowa City. Five-year improvements to make it their own that consumed a lifetime.

Now the names of Condit, Parmlee, and Sargent that littered the Scott County plat books and the great river shoreline would eventually be one.

But the best view of it all was from this second floor window and Condit shall still read on this deed until I take my last breath.

All Harry needed that day to put his solitary name on these plats was for his sisters to be gone.

Harry Deacon.

No Treat name given to carry on in Iowa. Things change. It was a new country.

No descendants.

No sharing.

All his.

He had lived to carry it forward.

H. D.

IOWA

the First Free State in the Louisiana Purchase 1673-1846

BY WILLIAM SALTER, 1846

To breathe the air of freedom, to live where labor was honored,
and there were no slaves, was the inspiring motive, more than any
other, which led the people of Iowa to make it their home.

Today, the whole world seems a much safer place, even as I lay here ready to depart from it all. Trouble is what Harry has taken to calling me, as if I cannot hear him. He cannot stifle me now. I can still find a way to have my own say.

Unlike Emma, I will not die keeping it all at bay.

Perhaps you now know this to be as factual as my Grandma Laura's warning when children tried to keep their secrets from the elders. The ominous power would come to claim us if we were to be dishonest.

Truth always seeks its own level.

Only a woman is strong enough to keep it from breaking surface. A man is less able to keep the demons or truth at bay. They eventually spill it all to save their own hide. That is what I believe and no one can take these words from me now.

Stoicism is not a female virtue, but a self-imposed penance. I will use it more like the Greeks.

My will is mine own. I have lived a virtuous life of my own choosing.

Yet, in a woman's strength to do so, to bring truth to light, she will pay an inevitable price that he will never completely understand.

The weaker sex.

The emotional one.

I can hear Grandma Laura now.

Truth be told or die in the keeping.

The Constitution of the United States

Amendment XIX

Section 1. The right of citizens of the United States to vote shall not be denied or abridged by the United States or by any State on account of sex.

Section 2. Congress shall have power to enforce this article by appropriate legislation.

Ratified by Iowa, July 2, 1919;
Ratification Complete August 18, 1920.

Emma always disagreed with Grandma Laura and countered that the truth be told never gave anyone any comfort.

Or strength.

I think it was the spring we moved the lady ferns from the riverfront to just below the sun porch. Secrets were best kept as such, she had added, as if talking with herself as we opened a rich bed to tuck in a tidy row of ferns trimming the front of Grandpa Syl's house with a false bravado of green.

Fiddleheads sought comfort and shade from and round the limestone wall and any crevice they could find, seeking coolness and comfort, away from the direct sunlight, like my Clara Belle's ghostly pallor she protected within the walls of our home.

Steeped as strong as the cohosh tea made by Mrs. Parkhurst and forced upon a woman when her child was emerging.

Emma and I harnessed the ferns into a straight row, teaching them to abandon the circle they would have otherwise formed.

Their only rebellion exposed as they found space within the spruce and fir remaining in the lots of our Parkhurst neighbors. Or creeping out of crevices, working their way through stone as thick as river ice.

There was a lesson here.

I would learn truth from the comings and goings of those around me. Real truth was to be earned.

No one was going to tell it to you in so many words, Emma had always said in her hardened way.

Without words.

Henryk Korn, Jr., had been county recorder and as such was responsible for the county voting records. Records mutually exclusive of one another as if the road record could not be tainted with the other resolutions and actions of the Board. But later also came the bridge book and the warrant book which chronicled the bridges constructed and maintained in Scott County, not a small book since crossing the Mississippi by bridge would become a relief to those who spent years crossing by ferry.

Henryk's penmanship was that of an artist and the minute book benefited from such a perfection of penmanship.

It had been his father, come from Pennsylvania to settle in the Gulf, who had so struggled with the language that he instilled in his son—the desire to perfect his English as a gift and an art intended to redeem the German clan's struggles against the conniving Irish and Scandinavian settlers who came to English with such ease, such unfair ease compared to the hard and cold word choices that he struggled with even into his days in county administration.

That German edge would never quite diminish, fortunately for him as the German clan was a united group and rested not comfortably and easily in Scott County unless a Korn held office.

Henryk Jr. had been a clean slate.

His father had sought to harden the boy the best that he could. Junior's endearing, boyish smile and his narrow, pale hands brought a warm tenderness to his mother but had infuriated his father Henry, Sr., to the point of a terror that his wife could never really understand. For it was she who wanted Junior to learn the piano and to take his charcoal drawings beyond their detailed parlor and express himself amid an ugly land where she had never felt at home.

Yet, his father would not have this as his legacy.

As Henryk's pen flowed over the pages of the county records with a flourish, he sometimes saw the flashes of the leather straps laid upon the backs of his six-year-old metacarpals, his wrists and on to his shoulders as he sheepishly ducked his father's slap when his A was not rounded to perfection and his B not aligned with the vowel that followed it, never protesting and always knowing his punishment was deserved for not being perfect.

It was these sorts of scars that never bled through to Henryk's artistry on the pages of the Board minute book as he transcribed the record that April day, the only acceptable art that he was since ever allowed to practice. I would be forever grateful to Henryk's beautiful manuscript in the official record that I requested at the service counter.

My mother, my grandmothers had never even climbed these limestone steps of the Scott County Courthouse even though their names were carved for perpetuity in the pioneer marble memorial displayed so prominently on its front lawn.

Unyielding.

Never quite knowing when it was time or right to give way.

Women had taken years to express an opinion in an open church congregation meeting, much less ever think of a day when she could vote for her own representation in a county ruled by the likes of those pious bankers, stubborn farmers and rivalrous river pilots.

My grandmother had egged me on.

I was sure of it. I could not have done this all on my own.

Mr. Korn's cranky records clerk tried to block him from my view as he sat in the far back of the open office space. As if the spectacles adorned by a gold chain around her neck gave her the perfect lens by which to peer down her narrow, yet flared, nose at me with disgust at my request.

Women can be so evil to other women.

It's likely one of the reasons this day took so long in coming, I could hear Grandma Laura say this. I coughed and raised my voice a bit too loud, showing them my nerves, as she also would have advised.

I paused as if I had heard her. Felt her calm hand on mine, and took it down an octave.

If you please, Mr. Korn, I would like to register to vote in the next election.

STATE UNIVERSITY OF IOWA

LEGAL AND POLITICAL STATUS OF WOMEN IN IOWA

DOCTORAL DISSERTATION

It has been seen that, at the beginning of Iowa history, the rights of women—especially married women—were largely fixed by the Common Law, which denied to the wife a separate personality. To-day, women may attend all State supported schools from the kindergarten to the University. They may also be employed as teachers in any of these schools, and the proportion of women teachers is constantly increasing. The professions also are open to women on equal terms in so far as they are regulated by the State.

Ruth Augusta Gallaher, 1918

My river is quiet today.

I see a lone, ragged oak branch floating along, creating its silent wake. Drug by a current that it cannot resist. Taken to a destination that it blindly trusts.

No escape now.

Surrender makes it an easier journey.

I know not how Emma carried and covered her way through each day, as I can only imagine how it must have felt to not ever have the outlet, the right to speak out about it as I am here.

At last, now I can be heard.

Silent shame can only be more tortuous than verbalized shame, more tortuous than the unconscious shame of my mother who never dared bring it into her daily awareness for fear that she could not survive it.

It is only now that I see what Emma must have so clearly seen and could not accept what she had become: mother, cow, producer. An atrocious female union of duty and obligation.

It was that outer tier of her face that I remember most.

The sharp, cutting jaw line that sometimes, yes, I felt I wanted to bash her heart against—cutting at the root of a misunderstood pain. She was a lexicon of answers for us, but only offered the

---

hard rock of womanhood that she clearly detested. So, we as her daughters dutifully detested it, too, until we had become power-less to change it. The second sex.

Resist.

In one clean instant, I now glimpse the hatred within myself for becoming like her, my own mother. Wondering whether it ever showed.

Stoic.

False pride.

I had worn it all too well. She had been a single mirage of false strength that could never be touched or relied upon because it was never really all there as we thought it had been.

I had so wanted it to be solid and true.

So I mimicked.

If you were to touch it, it would have crumbled into thousands of particles of a dust so soft and fine that a quick south breeze would send them floating three miles upriver, almost to Prince-ton, but separated and lost before they arrived.

Dispersed.

Never to be seen again.

So, I learned early on. Just best not to ever touch.

Commentaries on the Laws of England
Volume 1, 1765
BY WILLIAM BLACKSTONE

B Y MARRIAGE, the husband and wife are one person in law: that is, the very being or legal existence of the woman is suspended during the marriage, or at least is incorporated and consolidated into that of the husband; under whose wing, protection, and cover, she performs every thing; and is therefore called in our law-French a feme-covert, foemina viro co-operta; is said to be covert-baron, or under the protection and influence of her husband, her baron, or lord; and her condition during her marriage is called her coverture. Upon this principle, of a union of person in husband and wife, depend almost all the legal rights, duties, and disabilities, that either of them acquire by the marriage. I speak not at present of the rights of property, but of such as are merely personal. For this reason, a man cannot grant anything to his wife, or enter into covenant with her: for the grant would be to suppose her separate existence; and to covenant with her, would be only to covenant with himself: and therefore it is also generally true, that all compacts made between husband and wife, when single, are voided by the intermarriage.

June 1, 1600, Henlow Parish, Bedfordshire

All of her life, Agnes had diligently followed the word of her Lord. 1 Timothy 2:12 her directive.

I suffer not a woman to teach, nor to usurp authority over the man, but to be in silence.

She lived her days quietly under the mandate to follow her husband's every last wish, even to his dying days where he demanded she care for him as a mother would for a dying son. How odd that she had lived her life with this one man as brother, husband, and now like a son. Her daughters somehow understood, yet her only son remained disgusted as she doted on their father, keeping him alive with her decoctions of milk thistle and dandelion root.

Let the son o'bicchin' die, he told his sister.

If only he had been taught to respect his mother, common law or not, his sister later remanded her husband that very evening to teach their children to hold respect for their mother, if only in their hearts, so that she may never suffer the fate of Agnes nor their daughters hereafter or after that.

Her husband understood her fear, so did not suffer her for the unlawful temperament. Not this time. Yet, no dower right for her. But he kept that bit to himself.

It should have been little surprise when the pound came upon Widow Tilley's door that late May spring morning in 1600, less than 10 months since William's passing, and shackled her to a cart that already led Widow Johnson.

Why?

*Conjuratio*n, the vicar declared.

It was not the hammer that had inspired Robert's idealism, but the king's own words on the demons around us, within us, within others. It was all Robert had needed to begin his work and to give up his very mother as his first profitable find for himself and for his church.

Damn her for not remarrying; bless her for not remarrying, her son said to himself on her pre-trial day when most of his father's property finally became his after allocation of his mother's penance.

The judge had ordered her limbs to be bound and the vicar lowered her face down into the shallow water of the flood pond, the very pond that had saved her crop last solstice. This would be her last memory as she breathed in the darkness.

Robert had been wrong; yet, had she floated, his outcome would be the same.

Proprietor.

Father would have been so proud.

Innocent!

The judge cried, waving his right arm and pointing to the sky behind him as if in celebration. She is now in heaven with her beloved William and has been greeted by her mother, father, and our heavenly Lord who shall collect her soul for eternity.

At now 11 years, and old enough to attend the pre-trial, Robert's

•

son, John, watched his father's face as his grandmother was lifted onto the cart still wearing the mud veil. Widow Johnson had already confessed her covenant and willingly shown her mark as final evidence. But as assurance or deterrent, she was brought to the pond to watch, still shackled, and now drug herself to the furthest corner and hugged her knees so as not to touch the still-bound limbs of her dear old friend as the cart lurched forward.

John turned with his innocence to query his father.

Why did she not sit?

But, Robert was not listening.

Zenas ⎯⬚⎯⎯⎯○⎯⎯ Eunice

Sylvester ⬚⎯⎯⎯⎯

Washington County was God's country.

Great-grandpa Zenas told Syl so, and that is what Grandpa Syl told me. The families who settled a place like Prosperity, Pennsylvania, were as hopeful as Eleazer Parkhurst in seeing acres and acres of unsecured property for the taking.

A signatory to Damascus.

Work hard for the kingdom and it can be yours for a lifetime.

A farm to the eldest son. That's how it was done.

Yet, for Zenas, the church was always the real calling, complicating lineages and land records, desires and gifts.

The Pennsylvania farm went to Ira after Grandpa Syl left for his own wild territory parcel. Younger brothers left to find a trade.

At least one of them surely would become ordained, Zenas had said. Not always so easy when Zenas tended to cultivate hands over minds.

Cultivated minds did not follow his words so blindly, Grandma Laura had once hinted to me. Yet, he profoundly believed that one of his sons would hear the voice of God as he cranked on the well pump and the words would wash over him like the water washing sweat from his sunburned brow.

The Condit children of Pennsylvania had never been told of

the line that led back to the great awakening. Grandpa Syl had no idea that he, too, descended from the Rev. Treat and other unique presbytery stock much less its polity.

I only wonder now if this one simple fact of genealogy may have changed everything.

Land is better than cash in the bank.

Grandpa Syl once told me proudly, hands on his hips, as we surveyed the north 40 one July morning when his corn was almost thigh high.

He wasn't quite so declarative the next July when a sodden April, May and June left this field of puddles enjoyed by the river fowl and creatures alike making their way out of Wapsi basin and onto his tiny spurts of corn barely scaling the water line.

Grandpa Syl would be humbled by this homestead till the day he died on the 160-acre land grant along the river in Scott County. Land for the taking in 1833 well after the horrors of the Black Hawk War were done and natives were removed first to Iowa, then further south. More and more came by 1862 when you could carve out your own farmstead for the price of improvement, and posters back East said it loudly so many would hear a call to a glorious new beginning.

Fill Up Iowa!

Go to Ioway!

How could they not have come? *Emigrant's Guide* in hand; family Bible packed away with the English linen.

So Grandpa Syl packed up his wife and three-year old daughter and headed to Iowa for the free land and another sort of freedom that only distance in miles can affect. Miles and miles of freedom from Zenas and too far to hear his spoken and unspoken obligations.

Perhaps that was simply the liberty that Grandpa Syl sought.

By then, the Black Hawk purchase was filled with as many empty promises as the words shared with the thousand camped along the upper river when they arrived. As empty as the land covenant back in Pennsylvania that had been his birthright.

Ira gets the farm, Zenas had yelled as his parting comment, resentful especially in that moment of the son who was to be fulfilled in his image and was now fading away in his departure.

Pigheaded!

Would Syl ever regret climbing that riverbank and walking out the acres to stake corners around what he would deem as worthy of himself, his wife, his children? Perhaps it was never quite far enough away from a father who feigned disappointment, but all the while had openly favored Ira, the spitting image of his own father and a daily reminder of what he was supposed to be.

We are leaving, he told Phoebe one day when he had simply had enough. *Start packing.*

Syl came west the very day it was announced that the new land was open for the taking in 1833, that summer after the warring chief was captured and taken to the capitol in chains. Grandpa Syl loved to tell the native stories from back east, Emma had said. He would come in from a day with his father and remain in silence until well after supper. Then he shifted into storyteller and held Emma till she fell off to dream of natives and brush where her father as a giant lifted her from a cracking river ready to swallow her up forever. But we knew better.

On a November morning, Syl had walked into the Dubuque land office anyway, hat in hand.

Improvements, the clerk said as he neared the counter. Not a question, but an expectation.

Grandpa Syl had no value for the acquisition of dollars. His currency needs were defined by acres, sections, and quarters. He learned this language from the land office and began to share his

---

wisdom widely with the other settlers as they crossed the river to square off a parcel in line with their own new start.

By the time Zenas showed up to spend the final years of his life in Iowa, it was now a state where he could be near his eldest. By now, the residents of Parkhurst no longer believed that limestone gravestones were necessary to keep the dead from rising. The weight of the markers had been used to keep the dead spirits from climbing out from beneath the heavy rocks. The ghosts had at last moved on.

But no rock would keep Zenas out of his son's mind or Black Hawk's for that matter.

He never told me about the day the new singing plow was crooning along and hit, what he thought at first, was field rock.

The child's body still wore the fringed, tanned leather, and a smaller version of her tossed aside by a glinting blade, as if unimportant, like an abandoned doll's porcelain that late March day when ice was cracking and autonomy lay beyond the fear.

His pride had all been used up in fertile loam and steel until a doeskin dress had crossed its furrowed path. He was never quite the same about the land after that. We stand on their shoulders, Grandma Laura had said to us, but remember Grandpa Syl was not there that day. Perhaps he would have understood and been somewhat comforted by those words.

Moses' heart just saw it so differently. He was not so burdened, like his wife, by a lineage that came before him. He was one of many who were able to cross a river and leave it all behind. A line of demarcation. A daily reminder of when and where he had begun. Started over. No context.

A new sun means a new day, as Syl would say. A second chance, as if the first had never occurred. A redemption without the compulsory remorse. A penance redeemed for as simply as the slot that accepted a smooth wooden token at the Scott County Fair. Top prize.

No, Grandpa Syl was of another breed altogether, Grandma Phoebe would explain to us those times when he would tear up in a very unmanly way and turn away as if we did not see.

This was surprising for us from this sun-leathered man, more typically hard as the steel-nosed plow he so loved.

A giant to us, too.

Guilty for the asking. Guiltier for the taking.

God's country.

Independence Day Celebration

Black Hawk's Toast

I am now old. I have looked upon the Mississippi since I have been a child. I love the Great river. I have dwelt upon its banks from the time I was an infant. I look upon it now. I shake hands with you, and as it is my wish, I hope you are my friends.

Grandpa Syl always said that the summer before Black Hawk died, the river smelled like the dead fish of a wrenching execution, or as if they were the left behind from the rapture.

Dead on the shore.

Dead on the banks.

Dead to the world.

Laying themselves out in all of their glistening pallor and gore; drawing forth the mayflies from their early second hatch. Their brief lives made even shorter by an inability to leave their dying friends whose destiny, too, would be only a matter of days.

Time was up.

You could not go near the green tree without inhaling that horrible stench, he said.

The sight I imagined was much worse than any smell.

"Black Hawk"
Makataimeshekiakiak

"Whirling Thunder"
Seuskuk

Logan
(Sac name not permitted)

"Jesse"
ShahKeTo

"Mary"
Mesiconahha

People of the yellow earth, the Sac chief had said, this was our home. Our ancestors remain here. I can touch them now, visit them in the brush near the sacred river. They speak to me as loud as they did when I was a child and had no voices telling me not to listen.

Thank you for letting us return here to our homeland today.

We sat in our yard chairs, listening as attentive spectators to a culture we did not understand any better today than when Grandpa Syl had crossed the river. He said there were 1000 natives camped along the Iowa side, the land that eventually became our Parkhurst. Grandpa Moses had avoided this encampment by taking a steamer to cross at Rockingham, so never felt like he was moving in on anyone, taking anything other than what was his to take.

Probably the first white man they had ever seen, Syl always said. Even then, I knew this was not true, but would never have corrected him. It was his history. His guilt.

It was like viewing another religion.

Awkward.

We felt adrift without our own rituals to expectantly draw on or to draw from, but the odd phenomenon was that we did feel this spirit of which he spoke.

I remember seeing her for the first time that day when the Fort was 125 and we had traveled from Parkhurst to the island for the celebration. How odd we would celebrate such a fortification, a prison of doomed Sac and Meskwaki that had housed a shackled Black Hawk and sons.

Terrorists in chains.

Vacant.

Now more would come.

That's what I remember of that day. I recall those vacant eyes that did not wander.

When you finally accept you are lost, only then can you be found.

Her people said she was born with a second sight. At least that is what I overheard some Sac women saying about her, helping Clara with her plate as we gathered chicken and biscuits.

Is this what they eat?

I tried to quiet her and move her closer to their conversation so that I could eavesdrop. Prescience, someone had called it.

Behind the serving tables, easels presented portraits displayed of her in tribal regalia. I wonder now if she had known then that she was royalty. Great-great-granddaughter of a shackled chief.

Thunder clan.

Grandma Laura had said quietly to me once when I was reading a dime novel, and actually did not scold me for it, that squaw was a white man's word carried west from the bay colony and given to those who must spread, reproduce, and be shared to have value.

The childbearing genre.

They could not understand skwa and the radiant beauty of these female partners. They were not easily tamed like their own wives and daughters with commanding words, so they used the word to brand her.

Perhaps I had read that somewhere else as I tried to understand Grandma Laura's words, but of course it would be years and years later that I would recognize the important instruction.

Force is always used when no patience for words exists.

Retreat is sometimes necessary for us. It can mean survival, she had whispered.

I could not tell if she were speaking of us, the natives, women, Germans.

The other.

Years later, I would read in special collections that they had buried Mary in a borrowed plot from the Potawatomi in Tecumseh's cemetery.

Alone in a back corner, underneath the brush she could continue to hide her glory. Her own thunder.

Apart.

Her husbands buried with their nations, her children with their ancestry. She alone now, in this unmarked plot devoid of her heritage.

A princess who lived a 44-year life taking the most puritan of all names to her grave.

Mes-ic-o-nah-ha.

Skwa.

Oddly, I find comfort in such ironies now.

The New-York Times.

WEDNESDAY, MARCH 21, 1860

Rights of Married Women.

An Act Concerning the Rights and Liabilities of Husband and Wife.

Sec. 1. The property, both real and personal, which any married woman now owns, as her sole and separate property; that which comes to her by descent, devise, bequest, gift or grant; that which she acquires by her trade, business, labor or services, carried on or performed on her sole or separate account; that which a woman married in this State owns at the time of her marriage, and the rents, issues and proceeds of all such property, shall, not withstanding, her marriage, be and remain her sole and separate property, and may be used, collected and invested by her in her own name, and shall not be subject to the interference or control of her husband, or liable for his debts, except such debts as may have been contracted for the support of herself or her children, by her as his agent.

Not everyone arrived in Iowa by crossing the river.

Some had perhaps already been north or south and they simply kept making their way to somewhere until they came upon the village of Parkhurst and decided it was home.

Fill up Iowa! the poster back east had read.

The great river offered a natural boundary between civilization, better known as Illinois, and wide open prairies that would eventually be parceled into acres, sections, and quarters.

Iowa.

The posters had demanded it. Propaganda that misrepresented the harsh, bitter winters and the legions of drifts that were only stopped by barns, granaries and chicken houses that took years to erect and offered little to protect from a chilling wind that bit bone and tooth.

Wood-frame out buildings rotted in wet springs and then hard-baked by a summer heat only to stand proud against the next onslaught of a winter gale.

A few were surprised. Others knew it was better from whence they had come and no cold wind would blow them back.

Once, when I was twelve and had things pretty well sorted through by then, Grandpa Syl found me walking the Parkhurst cemetery alone to see that limestone set deep in the hill. Standing at a marker of one word.

BABY.

I am not sure if Grandpa Syl were speaking to me, but without looking up, I knew even then that I should listen.

Sometimes loss drives new meaning into gain.

Whether Asaph and Mary-Ann intended to be land barons or whether they simply needed more space between themselves and Parkhurst was anyone's best guess. In becoming a Sargent, Mary-Ann relinquished the Condit name with a relief and removed herself from the river crossers.

Born here.

Native.

Yet, it was seeing her name scripted on those deeds by the county recorder that fed her continued appetite for land as much as those grabbers and squatters of Syl's generation before her. She traced the boundaries of the LeClaire Township map with her worn, broken nail and underlined her name with an invisible line for emphasis.

That first time that Mary-Ann had pushed back on Asaph's demands was the first time she found she could do so with no resistance or battle.

A door was open. One whole year as a prisoner of war in Nashville kept him shackled to hope for Island City. She had supported what he had wanted and now it was her turn.

No wonder he so loved the structure that rigid confines and sharp-mapped boundaries can bring to a woundedness no one else could fathom.

Robin Throne

Pen to paper, Asaph had so swiftly signed the first contract with no opposition, no rebuke.

Mary-Ann Sargent.

Land owner.

Executive Mansion

Washington, December 6, 1862

Brigadier General Sibley
ST Paul, Minnesota

Ordered that of the Indians and Half-breeds sentenced to be hanged by the military commission, composed of Colonel Crooks, Lt. Colonel Marshall, Captain Grant, Captain Bailey, and Lieutenant Olin, and lately sitting in Minnesota, you cause to be executed on Friday the nineteenth day of December, instant, the following names:

"Te–he–hdo–ne–cha."	No. 2	by the record.	"Baptiste Campbell."	No. 138	by the record.
"Tazoo" alias "Plan–too–ta."	No. 4	by the record.	"Tate–kage."	No. 155	by the record.
"Ny–a–teh–to–wah."	No. 5	by the record.	"Ha–pin–kpa."	No. 170	by the record.
"Hin–han–shoon–ko–yag."	No. 6	by the record.	"Hypolite Auge."	No. 175	by the record.
"Muz–za–bom–a–tus."	No. 10	by the record.	"Na–pay–shne."	No. 178	by the record.
"Wah–pey–du–ta."	No. 11	by the record.	"Wa–kan–tan–ka."	No. 210	by the record.
"Wa–hen–hud."	No. 12	by the record.	"Tun–kan–ko=yagi–najin."	No. 225	by the record.
"Sna–ma–ni."	No. 14	by the record.	"Maka–te–najin."	No. 254	by the record.
"Ta–te–mi–na."	No. 15	by the record.	"Paz–iku–ta–ma–ni."	No. 264	by the record.
"Rda–in–yan–ke."	No. 19	by the record.	"Ta–te–hdo–dan."	No. 279	by the record.
"Do–wan–nya."	No. 22	by the record.	"Wa–xi–cun–na."	No. 318	by the record.
"Ha–pen."	No. 24	by the record.	"Aich–a–ga."	No. 327	by the record.
"Xun–ka–ska."	No. 35	by the record.	"Ho–tan–inku."	No. 333	by the record.
"Tun–kan–icha–ta."	No. 67	by the record.	"Ce–tan–hun–ka."	No. 342	by the record.
"Ite–du–ta."	No. 68	by the record.	"Hda–hin–hda."	No. 359	by the record.
"Am–da–cha."	No. 69	by the record.	"Koda–hin–hday."	No. 373	by the record.
"He–pi–dan."	No. 70	by the record.	"O–ya–tay–a–koo."	No. 377	by the record.
"Mar–pi–ya–tena–jin."	No. 96	by the record.	"May–hoo–way–wa."	No. 382	by the record.
"Henry Milord."	No. 115	by the record.	"Wa–kin–yaw–na."	No. 383	by the record.
"Chas–ka–dan."	No. 121	by the record.			

The other condemned prisoners you will hold subject to further orders, taking care that they neither escape, nor are subjected to any unlawful violence.

Abraham Lincoln,
President of the United States

December 26, 1862, Mankato, Minnesota

It was like that for Uncle Asaph.

The river had tempered his soldier's heart. Like the finest fishing line, stronger than its weight in borders.

Kept him in.

Kept him taut.

America's greatest public execution, I read somewhere later.

Duty.

Honor.

It was all good and right and just.

It is not God who determines a man's heaven or hell, Grandpa Syl had explained to me once as he scoffed at Asaph's desire to build an island city. Man's, he had said.

It was in one of those solitary moments, somewhere around that same time that Grandpa Syl had died, that I sat on a rough-hewn closet floor and cried over a painting, not only for these 38 hooded souls, but also for Asaph and his regiment.

A young blue soldier.

Exterminator.

It would be the 76 dangling legs at 5 after 10 that invaded my mind for years after.

Mrs. Arthur once told the whole class that my uncle had been a war hero. She had beamed at me so directly as if silently commanding me to beam back with a similar aura. My face and mind only responded with a deadness more typical of Emma than me.

We line the river bank, and Jesus washes us clean.

Zenas had proclaimed this when he saw the great river for the first time.

God forbid that it be so simple.

The Seventieth United States Congress

FLOOD CONTROL ACT OF 1928

No liability of any kind shall attach to or rest upon the United States for any damage from or by floods or flood waters at any place: Provided, however, That if in carrying out the purposes of this Act it shall be found that upon any stretch of the banks of the Mississippi River it is impracticable to construct levees, either because such construction is not economically justified or because such construction would unreasonably restrict the flood channel, and lands in such stretch of the river are subjected to overflow and damage which are not now overflowed or damaged by reason of the construction of levees on the opposite banks of the river it shall be the duty of the Secretary of War and the Chief of Engineers to institute proceedings on behalf of the United States Government to acquire either the absolute ownership of the lands so subjected to overflow and damage or floodage rights over such lands.

The river seems high today.

When they began to lay the wing dams, we all had a good laugh. Yet, we had laughed less years later at the lock and dams because they had put so many men to work that needed the work so badly, and the river had simply claimed too much by then.

Grandpa Syl would have laughed over the Corps' attempt to tame the great river.

A guaranteed channel.

Reliable avenue.

Don't respect it, and you won't forget the whoopin'.

He would have howled. Yet, he would have mourned just as much in his soft tough way as we helped our downriver neighbors to higher ground in the year of the great flood and those that had settled nearer the Wapsi as they lost their history to river silt and its lingering drudge.

That summer it rained and rained and rained, but Asaph would not leave his city. Little Syl vacated his home and moved his young family into dry Parkhurst. He threw up his arms at his father as the crest was only a fantasy and days and days away. He finally retreated from battle as he could not break through what he thought was a deafness, stubbornness and idiocy.

Hell or high water!

Old fool.

Homily xxxiii

St Gregory the Great, called Pope Gregory I
in the year of our lord 591 Anno Domini

———————

She whom Luke calls the sinful woman, whom John calls Mary, we believe to be the Mary from whom seven devils were ejected according to Mark. And what did all these devils signify if not the vices? It is clear, brothers, that the woman previously used the unguent to perfume her flesh acts.

Glastonbury, Connecticut, est. 1693

Eventually, the Treats and a small group of others departed the families in Watertown and crossed the Connecticut River to establish the village of Glastenbury.

Eventually they would give in and correct the spelling to its namesake, the first church in England, but Mary Johnson was not to be among them.

Dorothy Bulkeley Treat would never know of her husband's lost aunt. Dorothy had been born the year after the group who had crossed the river signed the act of incorporation, and proclamated themselves as separate and distinct from Watertown. By the time she named her youngest daughter, Mary, in 1709, it was well understood who her daughter's great-aunt had been.

After all, it was a matter of record.

A freed prisoner still carries the stigma of accusation. The suspicion of wrong-doing is a stain in itself. The shame of potential future wrongs.

A bad seed in any light.

She was not to be trusted.

They would say this to her grave.

Dorothy's opportunities were unique among all women outside of Concord. For all of the new England for that matter. Her father would come to teach her more than any woman should have known about the world of the unseen. Yet, he also overtly saw to it that she would never be called a witch, and a medical professional she became by wit and by blood.

When Mary Johnson had first heard what the men had proposed for the name of the new village, the old weakness descended over her like a shroud as if she still sat jailed on the dirt floor in Watertown.

The news had less impact due to the years that had allowed her to separate from the dank, dark walls of the alms house and the narrow walkway to Magdalen chapel, but the wood confines of the jailhouse had superseded those more peaceful days of solitary.

Public ridicule is always more painful than the distancing from family. The silence of an unspoken shame still manifests in all sorts of odd ways.

This was not a place she would ever go and, yet, she settled into surviving her days in Watertown, shunned by her own children. Loved by a foolish man who looked beyond her soil.

A lost soul.

Other than that short walk to speak no words with Rev. Bulkeley, she had not been allowed to leave the wooden confines.

Never even allowed to see her own daughters!

The last witch trial in Watertown had been in 1648 and Glastenbury was never to have a single one. The Reverend ensured both outcomes. The king's surgeon had certain influence and had helped the judges to see that unless there were at least two witnesses to each alleged event, then the event had not occurred.

A simple arithmetic. Reasonable and fair justice that could only be argued by a man.

The cleverness of the Reverend's logic was indisputable for many of the alleged incidents had been witnessed by lone individuals, many who were short-sighted women, so prone to error, they had posited.

The Reverend's argument had been very persuasive and Mary Johnson was not to be executed.

The governor and the Reverend had an alliance that was bound by the royal society of alchemy and with the Reverend's wife a descendent of Charlemagne. Well, all the better for rational decisions. All his borne gifts would thus secure his lifelong position and allow him to aid in the continued abatement of ignorance and fear.

The two-fold shield of religion and healing. The fear of death and the hereafter influenced many a villager.

It's a time of need for reasonableness, rationality.

The governor had told him.

Bring these villages out of their hysteria or we may never be seen as worthy of making our own decisions.

He had appealed to the right man.

The Reverend may have been a loyalist, but that did not stop him from noting each new and full moon, solstice, equinox in his monthly log. Pagan practices he would have otherwise condemned coming from a woman, but they had been long part of a motherland holy ritual that these colonists would never understand.

Literally incapable.

As a cleric-physician, he could be a man of science and religion simultaneously. No one questioned which discipline he drew from in any scenario. If a child was ill, they needed their doctor and probably needed their cleric as well. No one would argue theology on their child's sick bed.

He was the ideal blend of his passions and he lived in a time when he did not have to choose. So he alone decided for his daughter.

Dorothy pursued the arts taught by her father, but only after he died. Like all good puritans, he suffered from *misoginia* throughout his lifetime, but could not bring himself to view his own daughter with the same level of disdain.

His departing gift to her was a bequeath of equity unlike any physical property and money. In spite of all the years he preached for the godly obedience of woman as subservient to the men who lead them, their fathers and husbands, he left his daughter to think for herself.

Subservience can only lead to subversion.

He taught her these truths in private as if she were a boy and knew full well it could only be done after it was too late to do different. He would leave his library to his daughter and let her read for herself. To decipher royal society secrets never intended for the eyes nor faulty intellect of a female.

If there was payment for this in the afterlife, he would reconcile it there.

A library!

The barrister stopped briefly during the reading of the will as Dorothy exhaled the words in a moment of lost composure.

He paused politely as she nodded using the starched cotton to cover her shocked open lips, feigning an exultation of grief.

By then she was Dorothy Bulkeley Treat, having entwined the Treats and Bulkeleys in marriage to create the line that would find its way to create the middle land.

You would have made grandfather proud.

The second Rev. Treat told his son at the wedding held in the same year the official Glastenbury was born and years after the ancestor, born in Taunton, christened in Pitminster, and buried at Naubuc bargained away from Sowheag for 12 yards of cloth. No deed was ever found.

The legacy carried on from the blood of an Englishman turned emigrant proprietor. The new propriety.

His father was never to see his grandson, departing the year of the wedding, a grandson who was donned still yet another Rev. Richard Treat, one who had sealed the lineage of the Bulkeley arms and joined another Connecticut puritan line, the Woodbridges with their Yale heritage, and delivered one more Richard Treat, a junior; thereafter, naming his first son.

Ashbel Woodbridge Treat.

A Charlemagne-Bulkeley-Woodbridge-Treat, the ultimate puritan.

My great-grandfather.

Father of Grandma Laura.

My father's mother.

Son of an excellent stock.

THE REVELATION

OF ST. JOHN THE DIVINE

CHAPTER 12.

[13]And when the dragon saw that he was cast unto the earth, he persecuted the woman which brought forth the man child.

[14]And to the woman were given two wings of a great eagle, that she might fly into the wilderness, into her place, where she is nourished for a time, and times, and half a time, from the face of the serpent.

[15]And the serpent cast out of his mouth water as a flood after the woman, that he might cause her to be carried away of the flood.

[16]And the earth helped the woman, and the earth opened her mouth, and swallowed up the flood which the dragon cast out of his mouth.

[17]And the dragon was wroth with the woman, and went to make war with the remnant of her seed, which keep the commandments of God, and have the testimony of Jesus Christ.

October 11, 1957

It was the way back east in the Treat family that male children were named for their predecessors.

Paternal grandfather first names were often honored as a first born grandson's second given name as no one wanted to pass down the onerous responsibility of living up to the generation that had crossed an ocean or a river by saddling them with the forefather's given name that had led to a new era.

The paternal surname would eventually be enough.

The English days of naming daughters for their mothers were long gone. Instead, mothers' maiden names often found their way as the second son's second given name. Father's given names were usually the last choice and offered as a second given name to those blessed with a third or fourth son, although some rebellious son-in-laws may have pounced first to use it as the first name of a third or fourth son of his daughter, if the daughter were fortunate enough to gain such recognition from her father.

By our century, some grandparents would silently concede that a son-in-law had been in the family long enough to have earned this right.

In our parents' century, the new territory often forever burdened female children with their mother's names as their second given name.

This was my honor as Rose Emma Parmlee. Emma for my mother, although a mother I would never become to pass on the ridiculous tradition.

Please use no abbreviations and no pet names on the Parmlee mausoleum this time. Someone please tell the engraver to offer my full name.

Please carve it accurately: *Rose Emma Parmlee.*

It is all I ask in the end.

Let them know it was I who had been here.

GENERAL CATALOGUE

OF

PRINCETON UNIVERSITY

EST. 1746

TRUSTEES

Charter of 1746

William Smith, A.M 1748
Tutor Yale 1722-24; Attorney General and Advocate General New York Province 1751- 52; Judge Supreme
Court New York 1763-69; Trustee Princeton 1746-48, 1748-69; A.B. Yale 1719; A.M. Yale 1722; d. 1769.

Peter Van Brugh Livingston, A.M 1748
Trustee Princeton 1746-48, 1748-61; Member New York Provincial Congress 1775-76; President New York
Provincial Congress 1775-76; Treasurer New York State 1776-78; A.B. Yale 1731; A.M. Yale 1734; a. 1792.

William Peartree Smith, A.M 1748
Trustee Princeton 1746-48, 1748-93; Clerk Board Trustees Princeton 1767- 72; Member New Jersey
Provincial Congress 1775; Mayor of Elizabeth, N. J.; Judge Court of Common Pleas Essex Co., N. J.;
A.B. Yale 1742; A.M. Yale 1745; M.A.P.S.; d. 1801.

Jonathan Dickinson, A.M *1747
President Princeton 1747 f.r.

Ebenezer Pemberton, A.M., D.D 1748
Trustee Princeton 1746-48, 1748-54; A.B. Harvard 1721; A.M. Harvard 1724; D.D. Princeton 1770; d. 1777.

John Pierson, A.M 1748
Trustee Princeton 1746-48, 1748-65; A.B. Yale 1711; A.M. Yale 1714; d. 1770.

Aaron Burr, A.M 1748
President Princeton 1748 q.v.

Richard Treat, A.M., D.D 1748
Trustee Princeton 1746-48, 1748-78; A.B. Yale 1725; A.M. Yale 1728; D.D. Yale 1776; d. 1778.

They had been awakened.

It was not Yale nor Harvard. It was our heritage and Grandma Laura never let us forget that we as Henry's children had one-quarter Woodbridge-Treat blood in us. We were as much Woodbridge-Treat as Parmlee.

Richard Treat and Aaron Burr had sat at the same table, she would remind us.

She would never come to know all that I knew of the Condit side. More than one quarter. Closer to one-third in my estimation.

But no one knew, so it mattered little to anyone but to me.

I relish my imaginings of what Zenas would have done had he known that his presbytery roots lay at the heart of the great awakening. How he would have pumped his chest, projected his voice, had he only known that his mother's ancestor had been Richard Treat, founded Princeton, sat at the table with Burr and determined the course of his own Ten-Mile church.

Oh, how Grandma Laura would have argued this fact!

Do not disagree!

It was the red and gold altar cloth,

 I see it now, red for Pentecost, red for the fire that burned unclean within me.

The Condit Bible was always kept on the lower shelf of the book pedestal behind two small doors. It was the only possession retrieved after the ice crossing, when Grandpa Syl had gone back to the wagon and found it ransacked, almost empty.

Yet, the thieves had left the bookstand, probably because it was too heavy to carry away and the door within its base had been locked.

I can remember the day that I had found a key slot in the platform and had opened those lower shelf doors. I had felt like a burglar, a criminal, but had convinced myself that it was mine to read. It was my own history, after all!

I can even remember how low the sky had felt that afternoon when Mary had taken Lillie May with her to check on Mrs. Parkhurst who had taken ill.

I felt as if Grandpa Syl was looking over my shoulder and ready for a reprimand as I removed the immense and fragile leather from the shelf.

Perhaps I was meant to understand.

I knew immediately that it had to be Grandma Laura's Rev. Treat because someone had printed off to the right of his name: *the emigrant – Somerset to Watertown.*

Even then I knew the difference between emigrant and immigrant.

I knew there would be no reprimand. Perhaps Syl had always known what lay behind this locked door.

And that a key existed.

The Domesday Book

or the Great Survey of England of William the Conquerer
VIII. The land of St Mary of Glastenbury
[Folio 90V: Somerset]

The Church of Glastenbury has in the vill itself 12 hides which have never paid geld. There is land for 30 ploughs. Of this 10 hides less half a virgate are in demesne, and there are 5 ploughs and 17 slaves; and 21 villans and 33 bordars with 5 ploughs. There are 8 smiths, and 3 arpents of vineyard, and 60 acres of meadow, and 200 acres of pasture, and 20 acres of woodland and 300 acres of scrubland. It is worth £20.

1618, Glastenbury, Somerset

In an ancient chapel in the center of the small village, a baby cried. The precious sound awoke even those dying within the stone walls of the almshouses that lined the street in front of infirmary hall.

The rejection had come slowly for Mary Treat and most of the actual story she was never told.

Likely it was because she was from a good family and good families did not have daughters like Mary. There was no defining moment where she felt the shift from girl to woman. In contrast, the moment of dysfunction came quite suddenly and as quite a surprise.

Whore.

Harlot.

Witch.

There was still little tolerance for illegal fornication and the terms used to label female perpetrators had for too long been synonymous with those in alliance with the devil.

Not too often was a woman branded a strumpet that witch did not follow very soon thereafter out of the mouth of one good village man or woman or another. Promiscuity had been the consort's temptress and seducer of men since Jezebel and Delilah, and Mary had likely been a fourteen-year-old apostate preying on the human weakness of an otherwise godly Mr. Clerke. Especially when the clandestine was on holy ground–the parish graveyard was soiled by this evil encounter. The western circuit judge declared it had been, and the Reverend had even agreed with him. Mr. Clerke's charges of adultery were expeditiously dismissed and he returned to his faithful wife and children.

Children of these dalliances paid the greater price for the put-upon shame of silent glances; or even worse, the look-away whispers from the adults around them. At least other children were a bit more direct with their lancettes. Yet, the wounded child could never be the victor, so a solution had to be sought by the Treats in a plea to the Bishop. For there was nothing else to be done.

The Hammer had set the agenda for any investigation and was in arm's reach of this judge, but with no direct accusers and no desire or time to induce a confession, Mary's crime was conferred simply: illegal fornication. Yet, the punishment was never rendered as the vicar intervened on behalf of the family, and since Mary held no property nor was entitled to that of her father, the court agreed.

The argument was sound.

Consequently, she was taken to the site of the first abbey for she could not remain in the village almshouses. Although it was considered for a day, the Reverend finally said no. So instead, it was to be the site of the Lord's Mother's first church, now the monk's infirmary, where the poor and elderly men of that parish could find food and a place to rest. There, Mary was banished to the confines of motherly love that could and would cure her of her freewill.

As Mary was cloistered on the inside of the infirmary, she worked off her penance by cooking and then dutifully serving the meals through the small wooden window. She patched their clothing in the afternoons, and handed over the blue and white chipped bowls to the worn men as they lined up for meals. She was not allowed to deliver meals inside the almshouses to those most ill, but instead handed them over to the healthiest who maintained the task.

She may have been spared from execution, but not persecution. She knew her growing belly was her only salvation. Retribution was still necessary, of course, and extolled daily by Mary's own hand in the exile of her sparse room.

Her letters would arrive at Taunton Manor, delivered by a benevolent parishioner who delivered provisions to the infirmary once a month.

> *Regret torments me, Mother, as I stoke the fire in this place within me that I can now make hurt on my demand.*
>
> *Shards, sticks, slivers are easily within reach*
>
> *I use them all to pierce, prod and poke*
>
> *Seeing the blood brings me some comfort.*
>
> *Why did you take the baby, but not me?*
>
> *When may I come home?*

What to do. What to do. What to do. If only he had not taught her to write!

Mary's mother would pace the floors while the Reverend slept, never daring to speak of their daughter's letters (and certainly not her agony) to him who would only dismiss it with a wave.

Maudlin for a magdalen.

He would shout this in his odd way that no one quite wanted to hear.

Then, finally, the letter arrived that had quite literally answered her mother's prayers.

There would be no farewells when Mary was sold as a bride and set sail for the new world where she would meet her obligation—indentured for seven years to a husband's family in exchange for her passage. Her daughter was raised by the forthright grandparents who told the child when she turned four that her mother had died like an angel to bring her to them. For they were tired of the asking and wanted to be sure to tell her before someone else did.

What else was there to do?

The village talked of the disgrace for years to come, especially any time the Reverend's granddaughter was mentioned or a parishioner did not like his sermonizing. They knew well the mother been placed on a ship to seek further ill. Forgotten, but for the rumors that grew over the years.

A bad seed, they said, never produces fruit.

The girl was better off without her.

The Twenty-first United States Congress

The Indian Removal Act

Chap. CXLVIII.—An Act to provide for an exchange of lands with the Indians residing in any of the states or territories, and for their removal west of the river Mississippi.

Sec 3. And be it further enacted, That in the making of any such exchange or exchanges, it shall and may be lawful for the President solemnly to assure the tribe or nation with which the exchange is made, that the United States will forever secure and guaranty to them, and their heirs or successors, the country so exchanged with them; and if they prefer it, that the United States will cause a patent or grant to be made and executed to them for the same: Provided always, That such lands shall revert to the United States, if the Indians become extinct, or abandon the same.

May 28, 1830

When the wind blew the opposite direction of the current, Grandpa Syl used to say the river was going against its own nature. He would point out from his rocker on the porch facing the deep dark water, the darkest ripples over its deepest pockets.

Whose will is stronger?

I once thought this was his way to test me, but later realized I was no more than a sounding board for his own Zenas-trait, a need to hear his own voice rather than mine.

As much as Grandpa Syl was a teacher, Grandpa Moses was a storyteller. He would use stories of the natives to scare us into obedience. The fear quickly dissipated when Grandma Laura would walk in the room and say quietly, *We stand on their shoulders, Moses.*

Moses would ignore her, of course, and then continue on to wield his verbal weapon, searing us with tales of rampages, hostages, and scalps.

Harry would wail, then cover his mouth, cringing in the parlor corner, horrified. Annie would cringe with him, and I would remain seated on the ottoman, my ever studious self, as if this were simply another of Moses' lectures on east versus west, north versus south. There was always a battle line drawn somewhere in his story, and we, the obedient Parmlee children (the ones who had lived), were always on the good side.

The side of *right.*

Yet, somehow, I had listened more to Grandma Laura's voice on that particular afternoon. So much so that I would letter relate the same statement to my Sunday students at First Presbyterian, but would never have dared such an utterance at District 14. Public school, even then, was no place for diverse public opinion. Our textbook had said otherwise: *the government had been so good to savages, bringing them civility, education, and religion.*

We were never to learn the reasons behind Grandpa Moses' need to deify himself and use stories of natives to instill old fears in the midst of cultivated farmland long expunged of those who had once farmed it for themselves.

Grandma Laura's conversations on the matter were more private. They remained back east and left only to our imaginings.

THE IOWA DISTRICT,
OR BLACK HAWK PURCHASE

BY LIEUTENANT ALBERT M. LEA, U.S. DRAGOONS, 1836

Parkhurst.

Of this place, not yet laid out, it is sufficient to say that the site is beautiful, the landing good, building material convenient, and the back country fine. There is nothing wanting to make it a town but the people and the houses and these will soon be there. Its position at the head of the Rapids will throw a little more trade and storage there, than it would otherwise have. A good deal of the trade of the Wabesapinica will find a port at Parkhurst; and many persons, emigrating from Illinois and the Lakes, will pass by this route.

Parkhurst, Iowa, est. 1836

Mid-west.

Not east; not west.

The in-between place.

Moses and Syl had brought their families to the middle and had no desire to go back east or beyond to the unknown west. Having crossed the great river was enough for them, so they laid it down here.

Midwest.

More than a stopping point.

It became the place defined by where they had settled, not by where they were headed. They were to go no further. They would not look back.

And it was here they stayed to join the others before them who had persevered on their own to establish a village on this bank of a river that had belonged to others. A first cabin ridded of savages, as the president had called them. Moved them out, the cavalry had, and now it was safe and free for my grandmothers to settle their domestic wares. To build homes. To raise families. To harden their knuckles and their brows to scrub bare floors and bear blinding blizzards. To lose children in a quiet forest of red and orange glory not last seen since a new England autumn. Glorious was a Lord who gave them strength drawn from a river so rapid that they kept moving as well.

The thousand encamped in their midst till they were again re-moved to another in-between, this one far from the great river. Not east; not west.

Black Hawk's purchase. Section 85 of LeClaire Township was prospering. As it should, the president had said.

Then, when the followers crossed the great river, they knew where it was they had arrived.

The Midwest.

Iowa.

The new country had a center. It became a stopping point for those who could not or would not go on. Midwesterners: those who chose not to go further.

Thirty-Seventh Iowa Assembly

Babel Proclamation

The official language of the United States and the state of Iowa is the English language. Freedom of speech is guaranteed by federal and state constitutions, but this is not a guarantee of the right to use a language other than the language of this country—the English language.

APPROVED MAY 23, 1918

REPEALED DECEMBER 4, 1918

The Gulf, 1848

In every convex of people therein lies a gulf.

An expanse of space and time that creates a separation, a distance. A division that keeps us separate from those who are different than us.

The other.

To the south of my grandfather's Parkhurst settlement lay an expanse of land they began to call the gulf years before I or my sisters were born.

To me, it represented the physical distance we surround ourselves with when we believe our differences make us unique, unlike others. It is easier to shun those we don't want to define as our neighbors and can make their very existence difficult by our snobbery. Our visible disdain and dislike.

I could never understand if it was their difference in language or difference in religion or simply the food they cooked that really created the divide.

Silence as a weapon. It was just easier that way.

More civilized to ignore them.

Trees were used as the silent guardians of the division between Parkhurst and the gulf. Mr. Parkhurst and Grandpa Syl protected their village with this silent army: Walnut, Chestnut, Oak, Elm became streets. Suddenly the Presbyterians and Methodists got along.

Some think this was all about hate, but real prejudice can only exist within a deep-seated fear.

Fear of the other.

When the German emigrants became too many to count, Grandma Phoebe's discomfort in living so close to the settlement was apparent to everyone except her husband. This was so odd for a woman who had never complained about building a wood frame in the midst of a relocated native encampment or crossing a semi-frozen river with a baby and three-year-old. Only to bury that baby a few days after reaching the other side.

Get your husband to move you, Grandma Laura told her when she tired of her hypocrisy and her mimicry of language and dress.

He did it once, he can do it again.

We did not have a hand in that, Phoebe countered as if guilty over what they had done, having the first-ever argument with her daughter's mother-in-law.

It was the first cross words they had ever openly shared.

The English belong here. Besides, we were here first, she concluded her side of the debate.

It did not deserve a response.

She had learned the tactic from battling Moses when he knew he was in the right and no words would change it. No use to fight an unarmed man, she would smile to herself remembering her own father's words of wisdom. Yet, this somehow did not completely ease her mind when debating a misguided woman.

Unladylike.

Years later, I recognized they rarely spoke of such volatile issues to each other ever again.

Block 5 in the Town of Parkhurst

No. 4.

PHOEBE CONDIT (signs Phoebe Conndit) and MARY A. SARGANT and ASPAH SARGANT, her husband,	WARRANTY DEED.
	Dated: June 15, 1881.
	Ack'd: June 15, 1881.
	Filed: June 17, 1881.
to	Cons.: Other lands this day conveyed
EMMA PARMLEE	Rec'd: Bk 40 TLD 627.

Conveys the following described real estate to-wit:

Block No. Five in the Town of Parkhurst

together with   other lands

- - - - - - - - - - - - -

No. 5.

HENRY PARMLEE, husband of Emma PARMLEE, deceased, a single man, ROSE E. PARMLEE, ANNA V. PARMLEE, CLARA B. PARMLEE AND HENRY D. PARMLEE, all single, and heirs-at-law of said Emma Parmlee, deceased,	WARRANTY DEED.
	Dated: July 26, 1900.
	Ack'd: July 26, 1900.
	Filed: Jan. 18, 1901.
	Cons.: Other lands this day conveyed
	Rec'd: Bk 65 TLD 170.

Conveys the following described real estate to-wit Block No. 5 in the Town of Parkhurst.

ABSTRACTERS NOTE: The records fail to discole that any Estate was ever probated in Scott County, Iowa for Emma PARMLEE.

- - - - - - - - - - - - -

As the October chill meets a warm water surface, the steam hovers above a glistening current this morning.

The mist settles over the surface as if it is coming for me.

An illusion perhaps, but I could see Annie and Clara emerging from this cloud rising above the surface. They were coming closer and I feel their presence with me now in each of these days.

They are here with me.

I am not afraid.

My sisters' walks were so different, as if they each carried on from only one side of our family. Annie with her refined, graceful steps, mimicking Grandma Laura, and Clara with her clodding, almost stumbling, forward, like Grandpa Syl when he had scoped out a new clearing near the Wapsi.

But Syl's stride had led, and Clara could never really keep up with anyone.

I feel the sadness now as I remember how I used to make excuses for her awkwardness as if it were somehow a reflection of my own unworthiness.

Her walk on water this morning reminded me of how much I actually admired her inelegance. There was no pretense with Clara, only the simplest joy of life as she tried her very best to keep up with the rest of us.

She had so wanted to keep up and not miss out.

What was the main difference between the Parmlees and the Condits? I asked Emma as a delicate question once as I grew into a young woman and began to see the vast differences over similarities between her own clan and her in-laws.

The Parmlees paid their way across the river.

The Condits had to work for it.

But what about the Sargents? I asked, quite gingerly, as if she had forgotten.

They stole it.

The way she said it.

Felt like a rabbit run over my grave.

Columbia University

Consanguineous Marriages in the American Population

Doctoral Dissertation

In isolated communities, on islands, among the mountains, families still remain in the same locality for generations and people are born, marry and die with the same environment. Their circle of acquaintance is very limited, and cousin marriage is therefore more frequent. If we exclude such places, and consider only the more progressive American communities, it is entirely possible that the proportion of first cousin marriages would fall almost if not quite to .5 per cent. So that the estimate of Dr. Dean of nearly 5 per cent for Iowa may not be far out of the way.

George Byron Louis Arner, 1908

No one ever whispered their innermost fear at the first Wood-bridge-Treat-Condit-Sargent-Parmlee birth.

We welcomed each of Harry and Lillie May's children with a sigh of relief.

Normal.

No visible trace of too-close alliances coming to call on a poor innocent infant who had found his way to be born in Iowa through the three families who came to live together along the great river.

Midwestern was what they now called us back east.

Heartland.

Separated, not connected, by the massive coronary artery of the great river where Syl had found us a home. We stayed and became centrists of a sort.

Like some old county fair card reader, it was I who had pieced together these patterns. Forecasted a lot not worthy of Harry's children. My work was done.

I would never be aunt to these children. I had raised my sisters and brother and that had been enough for me.

We were now three generations removed from the desire to pick up and head west as soon as one turned of age and had enough independent means to join a group of other ignorant fools who needed out for one secret or another.

Jealousy.

Property.

Bloodline.

A common triptych that had fired up the soul of many a second son. So strong did it burn that he convinced his wife, from an established family no less, to join him on his go-west excursion. Convinced her that they would seek their own fortune, carve their own place from the future out of a blank land that awaited their mark.

They had crossed a great river and dropped their souls onto the hallowed ground they named as their own. Gave birth to a generation that would forever remain here.

Born here.

Native.

Mary-Ann looked at me with the relief of a grandmother unburdening her bundle of guilt, having carried it for much too long.

They were close. Loved each other always. As cousins, best friends. There were no easy answers on this dilemma brought from back east.

Genetics, they were calling it later on.

Through some science of blood and cells and tissue, that we had not understood until after we had blessed these cousins to wed, the weakness in the family trees may come skipping through our generation and showing up in the next.

We had thought it was safe and good, only to begin to learn that it was too close, too linked, like the Wapsi feeding the bigger river. The water-year you, at first, so rigorously fight until you learn to accept and live within it.

Lillie May finished her birthing years at three children.

It was all that had mattered to her mother. Once the fingers and toes had been counted, Aunt Mary-Ann always headed back to work.

10 fingers! 10 toes!

First Family

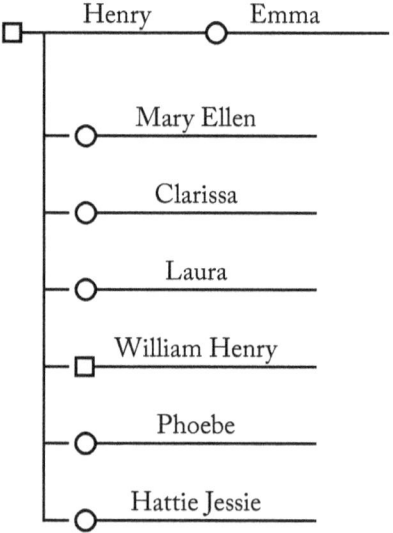

Henry   Emma

Mary Ellen

Clarissa

Laura

William Henry

Phoebe

Hattie Jessie

This morning I lingered in that place between sleep and waking where I could recreate my past and greet those who awaited me. I could have sworn that I heard Annie's voice or perhaps it had been Clara Belle. Their voices so alike.

Zenas was there, too, using his best booming voice to anoint me with two eagles wings and telling me to fly, as an angelic Grandma Laura looks on.

Such an odd dream.

I opened my eyes to the current hour, alone. Oh the comfort of an old friend, my sisters, who might as well be sitting by my bed, waiting till I awoke. Patiently waiting to greet me in this new day.

Take me home.

I whisper this now every morning that I open my eyes to no one but my river.

October is the month where I always felt better.

Pleasant hills, pleasant valley.

The upper river valley with all hues of yellows and reds and greens and oranges warm and comfort me along with this bluest sky blanket that wraps these bluffs like I used to wrap Clara when she was cold or frightened.

It is in this month where I always feel stronger. Year after year an inner sense has forewarned that something better is to come.

Something better for all of us.

Foolish at my age.

I am only to be reminded how foolish under this chill of fall that arrives when the sun departs. The cold will replace these refugees headed south, and when the lock and dams keep the water wide and open, the bald eagles will come to greet me and remain with me in my sleep.

Seems awfully fitting if this is to be my last October.

Diphtheria: Its Nature and Treatment

Without doubt, diphtheria follows general laws, and in many cases we are obliged to confess our entire ignorance as to the exact nature of those laws.

But if we cannot ascertain the influences which govern these epidemics, perhaps on closer investigation we may discover certain individual or hygienic circumstances which may affect them either as direct or predisposing causes. Thus, as a general rule, we shall find that diphtheria is more frequently associated with the ill-vented, contracted hovels of the poor, seizing by preference upon the unhappy subjects depressed by poverty and its attendant evils. Yet these are not the exclusive conditions for the development of diphtheria. We find in the various reports of these later epidemics that the disease has made its appearance, and carried off its victims, in the abodes of refinement and wealth.

Daniel Denison Slade, M.D., 1860

Grandma Phoebe had said that women were better suited to prepare for death, and birth. She declared this as though she were reflecting on the similarities. Our sensibilities are more fitting to it, she had told me as if she were my sister whispering a great secret.

Men should stay out of the room.

Hattie Jessie had been more beautiful in death than in life. That is what Grandma Phoebe had always told me.

A cherub.

There is a special art to wiping down a body and preparing him or her for burial, she had told Emma this as they prepared Hattie's little body and she had shared it with me one day on the river porch as she looked far across the water as if the scene were replaying itself as far away as Prophetstown.

It had occurred right here, on our side of the river, and just as destructive as on the other. Maybe it was easier to think of it as removed, detached, or separate from where the rest of us remained living and breathing.

I better understand that now.

The river remains unchanged, but our viewing of it makes all the difference.

Perspective perhaps.

A white muslin sheet from her bed was repurposed as a child's burial shroud wrapped so neatly around her five-year-old body. The christening dress had already been used for Phoebe Louisa's burial, and by the time she cut into her wedding dress for Hattie Jessie, Emma had long given up on the daughter who might wear it someday.

Diphtheria brings such ugliness to a child's body. It's the survivors who must return it to beauty.

Emma remained so held-down deep within her after that and no one could find it in her to poultice it out. When everyone finally accepted that she needed to keep it within her, even I knew it would never find its way out.

A handmade pine box to hold her baby girl. Wedding satin that had lost its hope and promise was used to line the sides to comfort Hattie with her permanent bedtime and her favorite prayer.

Now I lay me down to sleep.

By the time I arrived, Emma had forever descended into the non-feeling place. The fixed gaze. Ruminating hands that she could not keep still even in church.

I have heard that today's doctors may offer a bottle of valium for such postpartum hysteria, but in those days there was no such treatment.

Only a forever mourning.

Some sheep just stay lost.

Grandpa Syl told me this one afternoon as he watched me brushing my mother's hair right in the middle of the dining room. At first, I was embarrassed that he should have seen us like this, but then he walked over and touched Emma's crown so tenderly.

I held my breath.

For a moment he appeared to be Zenas, the healer. The laying on of hands was only for Ten-Mile Presbyterian, Grandpa Syl had said. He once shouted angrily in the barn to God after Zenas had offered a cure for Emma's condition. Grandpa Syl always thought he prayed in the barn alone, but we were usually there.

It seems we were always there.

Unnoticed.

The second family.

The good, quiet children who had lived.

H.D. Parmlee of Davenport Township Elected President of Scott County Farm Bureau for Ensuing Year

In other actions, an attempt on the part of the women members of the bureau to elect one of their numbers to the vice-presidency was defeated, 24-9.

Annie died more than 10 years ago now, and my Clara passed just three years after.

I had been alone in Grandpa Syl's house for almost a decade when Harry and Lillie May decided it was time for them to move in, which to them was the same as taking over.

Harry, who had always been a bit too buttoned up for the village life of Parkhurst had somehow up and decided to move his insurance business to town from the city. His three sons were now grown and gone, so he would take the old house now, he had told me, so matter-of-factly.

Almost as if it were his decision and his alone.

When I am dead, it is yours, I retorted. Equally stoic in my stance.

Such thoughts abounded as I watched Harry assume this new role.

The caretaker.

The last man to govern my days.

We both knew this to be true, but he had once made a cunning plea for me to give in and move to the old folks' home as so many of my old friends from the Presbytery ladies society had done in their final years.

Yet, there were so few of us left now. Mrs. Davenport had lost her wits and now talked incessantly to her nephew Horace who had died in a terrible automobile accident a few years back.

She would not even remember me if I joined her now, much less having nice chats as we await our passing.

The real fact is that I could not bear living with such a faulty reminder of time and place and the friendship we had. They called her a centenarian in the *Gazette* when they celebrated the century-old birth of a woman who lived instead from her decade-past memories, but as she blew out the one candle that also stood for the other 99, she asked the year and they had paused before they told her.

She turned to her nephew and said, Is that so, Horace?

No such luck, dear brother.

I will lay by this river until my last breath. I shall not be removed. That part, I would not say aloud.

Superior or not, Harry had his own troubles in Davenport and perhaps he sought refuge in Parkhurst the same way that his grandfather had once done after Black Hawk's war.

Harry had been wrongly accused of running a one-man church after a disruption over the firing of an interim pastor in the twenties, and then there had been that business with the Farm Bureau and the KKK in the thirties.

At least Harry had stood on the side of right in both cases. I had been almost proud of him then. So odd that he prefers H.D. now.

Harry had been born for these sorts of negotiations. He had always sought attention, and everyone had obliged him.

The influencer.

Always.

Especially the grandmothers.

Harry had never been motivated by the acquisition of land, property rights, deeds and sections, but of the dollar and all of the advantages he found it would bring.

By this decade he found his most fitting role yet.

The extinguisher.

Farming had never been a vocation for Syl and Moses. Harry could never understand that it had been their destiny.

The glorious fall would arrive each year and make all of the hardship and heartache worthwhile. The lift in Syl's voice and step in the fall makes me smile even now.

Harvest.

That beautiful, bountiful time of joy.

In fact, I believe I can recall Henry even touching me one fall. Why yes, I remember now that he had once even given me and Annie just the slightest of hugs!

He had taken each of us under his arm and tightened those arms around us.

I remember now how I melted into that embrace.

Melting into a desire for more.

And more and more.

Melting into the moment of relief that it brought.

A relief that just perhaps meant that I was here for more than embroidering pillowcases and scouring the cast iron.

Dare I whisper it now?

Had only I been born a boy!

But, no, it was to have been otherwise.

Harry had been the boy who had lived.

Second Family

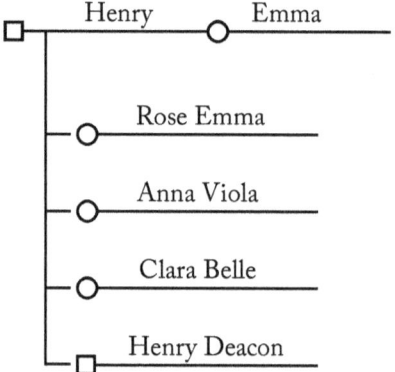

I remember asking to see my Clara Belle before she was placed in her box for eternity.

Highly out of the ordinary, Mr. Runge had said, but then he reneged when he saw the hole in my heart was larger than most sisters and gallantly allowed me into his embalming room.

He never did this for anyone, he gently reminded me.

I have done this work, too, I said as if I were his colleague and not a grieving sister who stifled a gasp as I glimpsed Clara on his table.

Not so easy, I added when I had caught my breath.

John Forest would have appeared so very tiny on this table that held Clara across what suddenly seemed to be a very long room. An ocean perhaps: water so wide I could never reach out to her. But then the image turned to the river and I was reaching; reaching across the rocks in the canal by Smith's Island, helping teach Clara to skip a flat, smooth rock across the water while Grandpa Syl fished for crappies and blue gill. The summers when he let us take our precious books below the tree and read and read until the August sun was setting, we knew he understood us, and we took our stories to an overnight with Grandma Phoebe in this very house where I write this now.

Clara was home with me in that moment by the river, not supine on Mr. Runge's table awaiting this closed box, beautiful though it was.

Cover her face with this, I said, handing Mr. Runge the Treat family stole (Lillie would not be getting her hands on this one) and I turned away from this ocean before I, too, drowned before my time.

A river began flooding the room and soon I would not be able to breathe.

She was my daughter that afternoon there in that long room that later turned on itself in my dream over two nights to be a Pelo's drugstore calendar of the numbered days, numbered pages.

Taught her to walk.

Taught her to read.

Taught her to pray.

Too short.

Yet, we had spent each one over a lifetime together. For surely this must be how a mother felt when a child passes before her.

Never alone till now.

I think it was that day in Mr. Runge's embalming room that I had finally understood Emma's distance. She had turned off the spigot to us because she feared her heart would burst, as it already had, and she had known no other way.

Instead, I had chosen another path.

I had left that spigot to run.

In spite of all warnings from my grandmothers, I had let it flow. And I had let no fear come to me that it would ever run out.

Oh, of course I felt the bursting heart, that feeling where death was always knocking, beckoning you to join your child on this table.

Take me now.

Take me instead.

Emma must have prayed it silently that day when John Forest lay wrapped in used muslin on a Connecticut table brought to Iowa on a dream and she could not make a sound.

The dream long gone by then.

I awoke that morning after Clara's funeral with no dankness.

No shame.

No bereavement.

No fear.

It was as if a lightness had entered me. Clara gave it so freely.

No pretention. Simply elegant love. And now she had left it with me.

A great gift that we could not share together. Yet, she always held her preciousness and no one took it from her. In many ways, her gift was what had healed me.

I always had that Condit strength to soldier through, but somehow then, peering over Clara's quiet face, saying a last goodbye, memory and lost purpose weakening every limb, I knew then that I wanted it more than anything.

Keep that spigot flowing.

Constitution of Iowa

1ST. Strike the word white, from SECTION 1 of ARTICLE II thereof;

2D. Strike the word white, from SECTION 33 of ARTICLE III thereof;

3D. Strike the word white, from SECTION 34 of ARTICLE III thereof;

4TH. Strike the word white, from SECTION 35 of ARTICLE III thereof;

5TH. Strike the word white, from SECTION 1 of ARTICLE VI thereof.

June 15, 1879

When Grandpa Syl crossed the great river, it had been viewed as a natural boundary between civilization and barbarism.

Yet, I was never quite certain which side had been which.

It provided an auspicious border that allowed for a crossing over of sorts, a departing of the old for the new. From danger to safety.

From bondage to free will.

How can you not help a woman alone with her baby when snow is as thick as an ice block?

Emma had asked me this in desperation one day when I was about twelve and I, of course, had no idea of what or to whom she was speaking. At first, I thought she had somehow emerged from her usual torpid manner.

But then I saw her vacant look and I may as well have been the moon, because it was not me she was addressing. Usually, I knew better than to engage one of these encounters.

It was so not always so helpful to play out these scripts with Emma. It had begun when I was about eight, so now I was an old hand at drawing forth the scenes from her mind. Even then, I knew it was not right to do this, but it brought me an understanding of my mother that I could not otherwise find. Perhaps I was wrong to do so, but I still see no harm in it even now.

A baby as black as coal and her mother, a smooth fine Lagomarcino's chocolate, Emma had said.

I stopped here. Silent. Waiting for what she would say next.

This was likely dangerous territory now, but I had never been more curious about what she was seeing in her mind's eye, so I could not help myself from this one.

Take them to the cave, she ordered me.

Cave? I asked slowly, delicately.

The cave under Mrs. Trombley's porch.

Hurry. Now!

Next door? I did not ask this aloud.

They will come for her tonight, Emma said in a careful hushed way to the wall by the clapboard. Drive them up to Low Moor, cross to Fulton, maybe Chicago, maybe the north country. To Canada.

Save that baby!

She screamed at me as if I were actually holding one.

Now I was scared. I had gone too far this time.

I had read about Mr. Scott. I knew all about what had happened to the Friends who had been caught in Salem and Keosauqua.

And, even then, I knew well why Mr. Lincoln had been shot before I was born. Why, I could even recite the Gettysburg Address by rote.

Emancipation Proclamation.

Yet, here was Emma, an iron-heart, trying to save a runaway woman and her child years before she could not even save her own.

Freedom.

She muttered this one word as if it were the answer to what ailed her. More like a pleading than a declaration.

Then, as abruptly, Emma returned to the stove to finish the cocoa frosting for my parents' anniversary cake. Forty-four years now since they had crossed and came together in this place to bear and lose their own children.

She never spoke of this again.

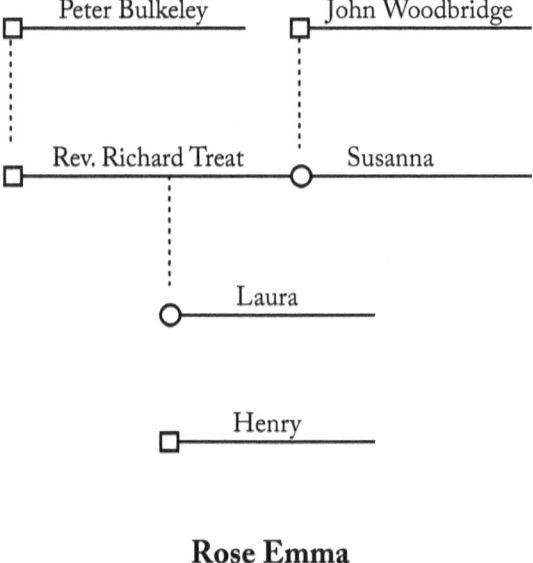

The day the package arrived addressed to T*he Family of Laura Treat, Davenport, Iowa*, Emma could not remember my name.

As she sat at the bay window that Harry had replaced last summer on the river side of the sitting room, she repeated again and again the names of her eight daughters as if reciting the books of the Old Testament in church school. Each time, pausing between Hattie Jessie and Anna Viola, but never my name aloud, the child that came between. The child who cared for her now. Wiped her face, held her hand. Perhaps it was simply not possible to acknowledge the one daughter that put her to bed each and every night.

Say your prayers now Emma.

I would tell her this, taking her place. She was me now. My mother, afraid of the dark. Places traded for good. Rocking herself to sleep. Whispering, I love you, quietly to no one, to anyone.

Like a rose, she said to me once, a play on my name without really saying it. She liked to do that and I played along. Like a rose, I would respond in the affirmative. She had almost given me her name first Grandma Phoebe had once told me, but quickly changed it just before my christening.

RoseEmma. Giving more than taking, but too sharp to touch.

I shook off the memory with a shudder and returned to the package's postmark: Salem, Massachusetts.

Some cousin of Grandma Laura's back east, John Harvey Treat, Harvard Class of 1862, had assembled *The Treat Family: A Genealogy of Trott, Tratt, and Treat for Fifteen Generations, and Four Hundred and Fifty Years in England and America, Containing More Than Fifteen Hundred Families in America...*

With a glance at the title, my theory through all of these years had been destroyed. Perhaps we were not so special after all.

Then a note dropped from the immense book's leaves:

Some families by the name of Treat are not included in this book, for the simple reason that either I had no knowledge of their existence, or because they made no reply to my letters of inquiry. It is my intention to continue my researches in order to obtain a fuller record of the family, and in due time to print an appendix containing such additions, and a correction of errors inseparable from a book like this.

The compiler is not always responsible for mistakes.

Please thank Laura Treat for her pecuniary contribution to my efforts. I incurred great obligations to produce this continuing folio, and it is through such contributions that it has expeditiously come to you:

LAURA WOODBRIDGE TREAT PARMLEE, DAVENPORT, IOWA, $3.00.

I turned quickly to the index of names that Mr. Treat had compiled at the end of his 637 pages, and there it was Parmalee, Parmlee, and Parmleee.

Then, just as quickly, I turned back to the C's.

Not a Condit listed.

Henry   Emma

John Forest

John Forest did not even live the full year of 1871. His life was measured in days.

We had named him John for the Baptist and Forest for added strength as Emma could not hold him, so Henry and I took our turns, and had the privilege of offering the second name.

I had been sent to help pick strawberries that afternoon. Sent out to pick while everyone else focused on their own tasks. No one would dare do such a thing to a child today.

It was just after 10 o'clock when something drew me back to the house, a dread that began at my heart and spread down to my fingertips.

No more picking.

It is surprising to me that I have less dread now in death coming for me than I did that morning.

I cared for her in that time as I would every day thereafter. Seems odd as I think back on it now. I felt so old, even then. But, I had seen Henry with the cows. I knew enough what to do.

Oh, how pleased Henry had been to see a baby boy when he shot into the house with a smile as wide as the Smith Island canal, but how quickly it was gone when he went to see the mausoleum engraver the first day that John would not eat.

It did not take long. Loss was something expected by then. At least the arrangements gave them something to talk about.

It was a better day when Harry Deacon came when I was 12. By that time, of course, we no longer needed a mother.

I remember the taste of bitter in my mouth and the pain in my heart when Mrs. Parkhurst actually had the gall to say I was too young to be in the room for his birth.

She can stay.

Grandma Phoebe had said quietly, but firmly. It was really unnecessary for me to be there as onlooker. It meant more that she had allowed it. Yet, I cannot recall how or why we named him.

All that seemed to matter in the days and years that followed was that Emma finally had a son who lived.

Her real work was done now. Yes, it had surely been my fault that John Forest was dead.

Zenas would come to see that, too.

At first, I thought Emma was simply chilled by a damp late March as the weeks went on and she kept wrapped tightly to cloak herself within her forsaken burn.

But by fall, the burn had been allowed to incinerate her beyond recognition—the kind of burn that does not leave scars, but clears a new space for an oddly distorted flesh morphed over the old skin as it consumed so completely like the purple loosestrife brought to Iowa by Grandma Laura for her garden, bringing some to Parkhurst for our gardens.

Tunneling from our garden down the path to Front Street, it became an aggressive invader and eventually covered the entire river bank below Front Street. A weed that spread a swath like the river flood, engulfing all else in a sea of purple flowers merging into a somber, amethyst carpet leading to my altar.

So beautiful was this smothering swarm ready to engulf anything in its path.

Yet, it remained the only altar where I could eventually purge my sins. A purple carpet that cushioned my knees, facing east, praying for Emma. Perhaps it was me and my selfishness that actually lay at its root.

Woman!

Zenas had barked from his pulpit at Ten-Mile High Presbyterian that was now our east river porch as he would read his former sermons to me, the ones he pulled from a hoary leather portfolio wrapped with a formidable strap.

Had they not seen this peculiar setting of a child on her knees in the weeds, an old scoundrel yelling from the porch, one might have thought he were still an exalted lay preacher giving it to a congregation who hung on his words rather than a four-year-old reprobate who hung her head and wished she could disappear. Rocking alone in the Boston rocker, he gave his performance until he was spent and needed a smoke out back. My wound could have been tempered by ash and exhale, but since not, I lipped his words in cadence with his rocking, arms across chest. I held myself in that loss and likely did ever after.

Another Condit son was taken from us today. The dragon had slain him before his first year. It is another sign from God.

He preached with such gusto.

Grandma Laura had told him more than once that I was too young to hear Revelation, but she was not here to silence his weapons this time.

Woman, bear your pain.

The stars beneath your feet do not protect you. Live with your daughters of Eve. Take their strength and for god sake, *give your husband a son!*

I had checked on Emma then to ensure she was asleep. Fortunately, she had not heard his harsh words this time.

I would bear her pain.

A Centennial Discourse
Glastenbury for Two Hundred Years
Entered according to an Act of Congress, in the year 1853,
in the Clerk's Office of the District of Connecticut

Ladies and Gentlemen;

Sons and citizens of Glastenbury:

My duty is to recall the memory of the past, that we may better understand the present—to remind you of the history of those men of fearless daring, heroic virtue and Christian principle, whom we are permitted to call our fathers to mark the causes which have aided, retarded, accelerated or modified the development of those civil and religious principles that formed the life and soul of the state which they begun.

Less than three centuries ago, and the wild man of the wood shared the lovely and the fertile valley of the Connecticut, with the wild beast of the forest, undisturbed by the foot fall of the white man, unknowing and unknown to the civilized world.

No sooner had the white man anchored his ship in the harbor, planted himself on the coast, reared a fort and mounted his gun, than the astonished natives cried out, MANITTOWOCK! — they are gods, and the fame thereof spreading throughout all the country roundabout, their alliance and protection sought by all the weaker tribes.

1648, Watertown, Connecticut

It was the *new* England.

Last names as first names, first names as last. There was a surprising freedom in declaring who you would be on this new shore, at least for the men anyway, as they signed the ship's manifest with a new version of the prior signature.

An *e* replaced an *o*; an *i* to replace the *y*.

Mary Treat carried the heaviest cargo to the settlement. Her modest baggage was outweighed by the heavy heart, cruelest to her sins that still haunted her when she was tired or let her mind sway and then it would sway the rest of her. But she planned to rid herself of this deposit as soon as her foot set on the shore. It was a new day after all, she told herself so again and again. New day. New life. New England.

Timber, timber, timber.

Move inland. Please. Move away from the cold harbor where mothers and brothers died in their arms, and they lost toes, fingers and hope.

For years in the new world, Mary thought she was the only one grasping. Clinging. Hanging on too tight. It was really the fear they all had carried with them. The pathetic, weak fear that took hold of the best parts of her resounding will that had survived that confined space, the suffocating walls that had been expanded to this boundlessness that other indentures called their sentence. Prisoners, we are, they had told her on the ship – those that she had dared converse with. Only the alms houses stone walls would ever again be a prison for her, stamping this so strongly in her mind that she began to wear a deep crevice midbrow, a valley that had belied her youth.

No one in Watertown would know that the hard-working, strong-willed Mary Johnson had once been the unchaste Mary Treat, except of course, the Reverend Treat and his wife as they arrived one day to the Watertown colony and were aghast to see their daughter as a grown mother of three of her own: Prudence, Mercy and Hope. So named so perhaps her daughters would live out the sentiments she had missed. Greeting their granddaughters like strangers, the Treats held their sharp chins high and cold and Mary was only able to release her inner clapboarded sweet bitter thanks to the herbal balm from Goodwife Harrison. Hushed her, calmed her, actually soothed her, at least soothing the quaking in her knees.

No one knows here, she said silently. No one knows. Her mind raced with a fantasy of playacting, sin or not, she acted out the ideal scene in her mind. Could we not be long lost cousins? Could you not rush at me, sweep me up, embrace me? Claim me? At least show that we are connected? Are we not connected?

We are not connected.

It was foretold in the quickness of her mother's glance away to avoid her direct gaze and jarred Mary out of this self-indulgent daydream. We were not connected as she herself diverted her gaze to her own feet, foreign they seemed in this moment, somewhat old. The old shame revisited with a full gale. It took a shudder of her shawl to squelch the urge to dash to the river and immerse herself in the dark water.

She looked over at her husband, Oliver, greeting the newcomers who had found their way, and somehow the courage to leave Barnstable and join the Connecticut purest of the pure. Oh, Oliver. If he only knew that his orphan virgin bride—paid for with an Atlantic passage—had actually been raised at Tauton Manor and had used all their credits with the bishop to salvage her pitiful and useless existence.

Have I returned my board, husband?

Thinking of yourself again?

The uninvited mind talk spanked her rudely back to hear the hearty and grandest greetings Oliver gave to these grandparents of his own daughters, soon to be wed themselves, never knowing they were the Harvard Treats of the bay colony. Only later she would be certain to tell the girls all the godly reasons for why confidence was not a sin and the strongest females bore males.

Hold your heads high! You will have sons!

But then, perhaps a moment of recognition! The youngest woman in the Treats' party extended her hand to Mary Johnson and she allowed herself to connect in an intoxicating gaze with the daughter she would never know.

My name is Honour, she had said.

Fear is weak.

Truth cannot be unbroken, only untruth.

It is so oddly disturbing just when and where one is when memory finds its way to the mind's eye. How can all of the good years not erase so few bad, Mary queried, holding her jaw tight, forcing the images of her grandchildren to override the mind, marching them through in the order of their birth, again and again, as she waited on the floor of a wood-framed cell this time. But the trick failed her since her daughters were now as ashamed of their mother as her own mother had been the day of her village arrival. Their faces blurred their children.

I want to see the prisoner.

Reverend Bulkeley ordered the jailer. He was so tired. Tired of these greedy self-appointed judges who so easily gathered this woman's property up for distribution now that her husband was gone to garner it for themselves in the name of the law or redistribute to the deserving family. He had seen it in the commonwealth and now here it was again. The governor would help him see to it that no more women were racked and burned in the name of this ridiculous charade. Keep them from turning to the barbarism of rogue island was all the king's agent had said. Do what you will, but keep them under the crown and we will continue your status in the royal society.

Mother says you find such relief in conflict, Oliver had once declared in a tone that bit her in that old place. She dared never to ask for clarification from the one man who had stood by her, in spite of his mother's disapproval in his choice of a bride. Till his death from the pox, he stood by her. There were no balms for the pox, but Oliver was the one she could feel with her now.

At least she had that.

I see red
Circles of light
Weaving shards of sadness
Move along now
Moving through
Held too long
In that secret holding place
Too tight
Let go
Move through alone
It no longer belongs here.
Light a flame for the passing.
Holy, Mary Magdalen, pray for me.

The learned and privileged stoic men who had built Watertown did not always feel their daughters were capable of intellectual pursuits. It simply was not possible for their gender. Yet, in this case, the words were somehow dismissed as magic and blasphemy, so even more easily discounted.

Like the women in Solomon's kingdom, if language served the lesser gender, they were somehow lost to demons.

Only the Wisdom could share words worthy of capture as *Psalms* and use a female pronoun as God. It was like the spirit of the sea, ethereal not corporal. Like the ignorant wordplay of children, puritan women were better kept silent.

Their gibberish meant nothing.

Three decades and Mary had just not learned. She had not changed in the new England any more than she had in the former. After all she had been through and she still could not keep her wicked thoughts to herself.

So, an actual witch or not, the punishment was just.

Rev. Treat, a pristine village elder with no shame upon him, once again tossed aside the words of his only daughter's poetry when the jailer handed him what appeared to be a simple missive from the captive to her children.

Better off without her.

THE REVELATION

OF ST. JOHN THE DIVINE

———————

CHAPTER 20.

¹²And I saw the dead, small and great, stand before God; and the books were opened: and another book was opened, which is the book of life: and the dead were judged out of those things which were written in the books, according to their works.

Words are things.

I see this truth so clearly now, but I had read this so long ago now. Was it Lord Byron? Grandma Laura would be so disappointed in me that I cannot now recall. My mind is slipping.

Words are the only connection I have here to reconstruct these memories and their relations. To make meaning of it all.

We are all connected. I am as sure of it now as Emma was.

Yet, for my sake, I must more than know it. I must make sense of it. I do not accept so easily what is told to me. This my downstairs captors know for sure.

Such beautiful instruments they have brought me to aid my hands in this final work, feigning ignorance to my writing. Capturing these things with graphite and linen allows me to bring them to the light in such a beautiful manner. Artistic.

Bring them out as I see them.

Where I can see them.

There is nothing left to fear now.

Perhaps, in the end, Zenas had it right after all.

They need to be put out.

Put down.

The things must be left behind.

SOCIAL STATUS, MEASURED INTELLIGENCE, ACHIEVEMENT, AND PERSONALITY ADJUSTMENT OF RURAL IOWA GIRLS

By Lee G. Burchinal, Iowa State College

The data were based upon test responses from 176 girls who were in the fourth through the tenth grades in four rural schools in a central Iowa county in the spring of 1956. Families were predominantly second or third generation American. Very little or no relationship was found between the father's occupation, education of the father or mother, family social status and female academic achievement and personality adjustment.

I almost missed out on a secondary education much less a post-secondary one.

Girls are not equipped for higher learning.

I could only dream a frustrated dream of resistance, but thanks be to God and Grandpa Syl who encouraged me to read.

Yes, I could read.

And it had been Grandma Laura's reading list that brought me through the threshold that only my grandmothers had imagined for me, reconstructed from their own lost futures when they headed west with their husbands and young children. Their own fathers had seen to that.

If Grandpa Moses had his way, my lot would have mirrored theirs and my mother's.

Marriage.

Children.

Grandchildren.

These were to be the generational joys of life for women in my family. There was nothing more for which to be thankful or to yearn as long as you had your husband, your home, and your children.

Fortunately, Grandpa Syl had intervened.

For the first time ever, on any matter, he sided with Henry and defended his wishes to his daughter's father-in-law on my behalf. This had never happened on property, boundaries, events. Only for me.

For Lord sakes!

Grandma Phoebe had unashamedly exclaimed to me and Emma. Although, of course, she knew Emma wasn't listening, so perhaps her glee was for my ears only. Or perhaps her shouts over her daughter's success may have perked an interest in the silent Emma, but it was not to be. Lighter words were all that piqued her mind these days—the blooming of the wild roses on the trellis beneath the river porch.

But a Condit girl to pursue a secondary education: not an inkling of acknowledgement nor word was spoken.

'Tis not a *higher* education, simply a necessary one, Grandma Laura corrected her despite her agreement in the gloried news. She, too, had fought her husband on this one.

Pick your battles.

She had always advised me, and for this one, she had decidedly joined forces with Grandpa Syl.

The Condits and Parmlees in agreement was a phenomenon. It was a new day. One she knew she would likely pay for in these final years with her husband, but she cared not as her own retaliation would prevent it from becoming too severe.

I am a Treat. We teach our girls.

Grandma Laura had reminded them of this truth when only

females were gathered in the kitchen, a rare gathering of the two families preparing a meal together that typically had never happened unless it were a birth, wedding, or a death.

I pondered on this significance and knew better than to think this was all about me and my attendance at Miss Ira's School for Girls that fall.

Let the Parmlees do as they will, but this Treat grandchild will be educated beyond grade school, Grandma Laura boasted of the command she had given to Moses, but kept the actual coercive details to herself.

You cannot discount her potential. It is obvious to all of us.

I cried alone over this more than once as I had watched Harry graduate from the Davenport high school and then from the Iowa state college.

No Ivy League for the Iowa boy. A land grant college gave the first Condit-Parmlee, river crossers, to achieve this now or even before. So everyone thought.

Harry was better suited for higher education, for intellectual pursuits as Grandpa Moses termed them when he won the final battle as I graduated from Miss Ira's and made my plans for Iowa college.

Of course, it sounded sweet, but it would not be.

Women were just not suited, I had been reminded.

I was 16 when Mrs. Collier handed me my diploma. I felt finally grown, but never doubted then that I would eventually marry, have children, enjoy my grandchildren.

Of course, that too, would not be.

Yet, my yearnings were never so tumultuous as when I read the *Gazette* and secretly cheered for those first women who attended the college. My secret sisters that kept me from looking aghast at what my own life had become.

Unmarried.

Head of household.

Spinster.

By 50, it was who and what I had become.

By 90, I am grateful.

It was only by women I had felt most judged for remaining this unmanaged, undesirable form of a woman.

Once my grandfathers and my father were gone, I had no man to direct my life. My decisions, to pay my taxes, my insurances, were mine. I alone directed the important decisions of my life and those of my sisters.

Yet, somehow, within, I never felt as unwanted as they would have had me believe.

Moses had tried to start a school once in Davenport when your father and his brothers were young, Grandma Laura confided in me one May day, years after it was very clear that I would not be on any path to formal higher learning. She shared the clipping from the *Gazette* that described the school that had lasted just one academic year.

The audacity.

Crossing rivers and prairies to become a farmer's wife could never purge the Harvard-Yale-Princeton Woodbridge-Treat blood from her veins.

Land grants are for those who use their hands instead of their brains.

I had to smile with her.

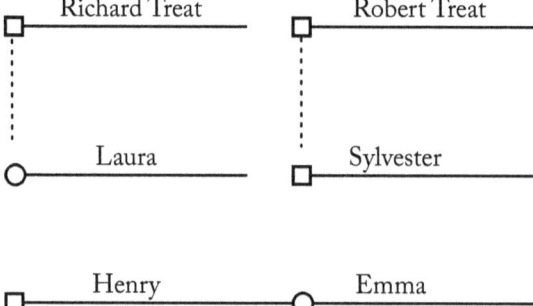

Richard Treat

Richard Treat   Robert Treat

Laura   Sylvester

Henry   Emma

Rose Emma

Crossing a river was nothing compared to crossing an ocean.

Crossing the ocean had been a break as loud as an independence day fireworks celebration, a break in the bondage to a homeland that never really let its children completely grow up, be free. Think for themselves.

The answer was always simpler than the action.

Leave.

But once on new soil, a new ground, the generational shift always occurred and children became bound once again to a redefined sense of heritage, security. The place of family and history that was place bound.

Only the bravest would decide to leave it again.

Ashbel Woodbridge Treat was once part of the great rebellion as he brought together the Treats, the Bulkeleys, and the Woodbridges, three English lines into a single American man who fought for a freedom from a sovereign and won.

A freedom taken by geography an ocean apart.

Ashbel needed the unbounded promise of the new territory. Yet, when opportunity arose, he could not leave the east. Thinking on it in the warm dank evening of an independent memory of a promise made in a dark underbrush surrounded by the king's men who could not see him.

He swore to never leave.

Here it was he had fought, survived, married, and would die—buried on his own parcel, leaving it to his children who would remain. This was not the Connecticut land of his grandfathers, but that of his own making. The new York. He had lived through it, so he would stay put now that he had made this safe ground.

Surprising to everyone except maybe those who knew her best, it was to be his daughter, Laura, who would go west. A Woodbridge-Bulkeley-Treat turned Parmlee for an unfounded reason. Her justification she would never explain.

Laura would follow Moses as if he could part the sea, and she would take the east with her.

She would begin anew.

Unbounded.

She crossed a great river and landed safely home. Her reasons remained her own.

The Extra Session of
the Twenty-sixth General Assembly of the State of Iowa

Whereas, the Executive Council has authorized the wild rose of
Iowa as one of the decorations on the silver service presented to
the battle ship Iowa; therefore be it

Resolved, by the Senate, the House concurring, That the wild rose
shall be officially designated as the flower of the State.

CONCURRENT RESOLUTION MAY 7, 1897

After the great glacier had receded and the ice melted, the river valley was formed. The finest of materials migrated into the valley and the persistent stream became a great river surrounded by the richest of soil from which civility was born.

I saw the sky in the river this morning.

No one owned the river, Black Hawk said as if he whispered in my ear.

Or is it my grandfather here to join me now? Their words seem so similar at this early hour.

Clouds reflecting on to the water, as if they are moving across the man-carved channel guaranteed at nine-feet as only engineers can assure. Yet, no one can guarantee delivery of a clear sky.

This day is my prayer.

Sea to sky.

Sky to sea.

As if one were a reflection of the other.

One moving, parallel to another, and one as still as the handheld mirror turned upward on my dressing table that I can no longer reach. Not that I want to see what it reflects back to me, but it is the reaching that I still pray for, as the reaching is what keeps me hopeful.

Who is to say which is what.

What would I see if I could reach across the room and grasp that mirror now? What are final days of a life if not given to contemplation, reflection, a path to meaning.

Regret.

What was it Emma had said about crossing the river?

Everyone became your family then.

I wonder sometimes now if it is like that when we cross over. Where is your family when one feels so very alone on this day counter to your birth?

The other side of this very long journey.

As Mr. Twain told us, when Mr. deSoto first saw the great river, he was so taken that he died on the spot, and was rolled into a carpet and dumped in the river by his priests and soldiers. Fortunately, for me, I have enjoyed this masterpiece a bit while longer and without such hysterics that are more typically blamed on women.

This I know now for sure. The joy plus the sad is what makes us real.

We cannot separate ourselves from what is our own,

what made us,

what brought us here.

No one can escape the sad if they seek the good.

It may recede, yet always returns like the river does, always finding its own way.

Such vanity visits me in this final hour.

Will anyone care on Sunday morning when I don't take my pew? Will they even remember who used to sit there eight minutes to eight, smiling at babies and sisters and lifelong friends now long gone before me?

Who will cry at my funeral?

I have no children or grandchildren to surround me. My property has already been signed to my brother, my nephews. Let them pick and fight over what they perceive of value.

I say, shame on them for giving me no grandniece to carry on this beautiful name!

When they read my name on the Parmlee mausoleum, will those years carved with such care have meant something? Will these words explain? Will they know I was always more of a Condit-Treat than ever a Parmlee-Treat?

I will reside there soon enough now with my dear sisters, John Forest, and the first family, gone on too soon before me. And Emma and Henry: brought to Iowa on someone else's dream. A dream that for them turned to an infinite grief with each passing child.

Yet, somehow they bore on.

How odd that I see a mourning dove at my window. It must be near time now.

I found no husband in my day to lay down by my side. No children at my feet. Harry and Lillie May will not join us. They will have their own plot soon enough to lay out their children and grandchildren and great-grandchildren.

Yet, only if the generations remain here.

Some of them may have their own dream of moving on. Some will know there is always something better than what our parents and our grandparents willed for us.

Others will inherit the magnanimous and infectious spirit of Grandpa Syl and take a journey across land and water to carve out his own resolve of his own making on his own terms, and some will possess Emma's strength to carry on in spite of it all.

Still others will pass long before they are ready, and others will use that long slow time to reflect as I have here.

I pray now for all of them that they may find their own crossing.

My sweet Lord, I have no secrets left to share, and please remember me, my dear great river.

For *I was here!*

Davenport Gazette

The Half Century Issue, 1855-1905

by Mary E. Parkhurst, 1905

Parkhurst is no longer a city but a peaceful, restful village of 800 inhabitants. Many of her industries have crumbled before the stern and relentless tread of Time, yet with the many beautiful homes, town hall, school building, churches and public-spirited citizens prosperity and happiness may ever await the guardian angels at her gateway. She is no longer isolated for the railroad and interurban have linked her with the great outside world, of which she is a beautiful and symmetrical part. The Condit-Parmlee family are the only living who have had a continuous residence in Parkhurst since the Black Hawk War as Miss Rose Parmlee and her sisters maintain the original Condit family home on River Road. Their parents and grandparents were among the first to cross the great river and settle what was to become our glorious state.

Ask Me

Some time when the river is ice ask me
mistakes I have made. Ask me whether
what I have done is my life. Others
have come in their slow way into
my thought, and some have tried to help
or to hurt: ask me what difference
their strongest love or hate has made.

I will listen to what you say.
You and I can turn and look
at the silent river and wait. We know
the current is there, hidden; and there
are comings and goings from miles away
that hold the stillness exactly before us.
What the river says, that is what I say.

William Stafford

Acknowledgments

Even though a work of literary fiction takes many liberties, the story of Rose Emma was inspired by true events of the great migration. The journey to assemble Rose's manuscript was a long one for such a minimalist work. I am indebted to an incredible creative team without which this story would not have seen print: Sarah, Burton, Kristin, and Pratt; the Midwest Writing Center and the LeClaire Writers for their singular encouragement: keep writing; Professor Glenda Riley for her inspiring alternative texts on pioneer women; Jotham Halsey and Ebenezer Condit for their genealogy of the Condit family; John Harvey Treat for his genealogy of the Treat family; writing and research spaces like The Writers' Well, the Sea Islands, Scott County and the city of LeClaire, especially the courthouse, libraries, historical societies, and the Buffalo Bill and Putnam Museums; the great river; and mostly to Rose and Emma, I will always remember.

CASLON

Created in 1722, Caslon was the first major typeface to be used for the English language. It continued to be the dominant type in the American colonies in the second half of the 18th century. Recognized for its slightly bracketed serifs and old-style irregularity, Caslon maintained its popularity when Carol Twombly created Caslon for Adobe in 1990.